WHEN THE LAST LEAF FALLS

By Bill Myers

Blood of Heaven
Threshold
Fire of Heaven
Eli
McGee and Me (children's book/video series)
The Incredible Worlds of Wally McDoogle (children's comedy series)
Blood Hounds Inc. (children's mystery series)
Faith Encounter (teen devotional)
The Dark Side of the Supernatural

Novellas
Then Comes Marriage (with Angela Hunt)
When the Last Leaf Falls

When the Last Leaf Falls

a novella

BILL MYERS

GRAND RAPIDS, MICHIGAN 49530

ZONDERVAN™

When the Last Leaf Falls

Requests for information should be addressed to:
Zondervan, *Grand Rapids, Michigan 49530*

Library of Congress Cataloging-in-Publication Data
Myers, Bill, 1953–
When the last leaf falls / Bill Myers.
p. cm.
ISBN 0-310-23091-8
1. Terminally ill—Fiction. 2. Grandfathers—Fiction. I. Title.
PS3563.Y36 W48 2001
813'.54—dc21 2001026317

This edition printed on acid-free paper.

Published in association with the literary agency of Alive Communications, Inc., 7680 Goddard Street, Suite 200, Colorado Springs, CO 80920.

Interior design by Melissa Elenbaas
Printed in the United States of America

01 02 03 04 05 06 /❖ DC/ 10 9 8 7 6 5 4 3 2 1

In memory of Bill Myers Sr.

1919–2000

a man of simple greatness and faith.

This one's for you, Pop.

"We have here only five loaves of bread and two fish," they answered.

"Bring them here to me," he said.

Matthew 14:17–18

THE PHONE HAD BARELY CHIRPED BEFORE I HAD THE RECEIVER to my ear. "How is she?" I asked.

"They said . . ." Jen took an uneven breath and my heart stopped. I searched for the slightest clue in my wife's voice, in the way she hesitated, in the way she breathed. At last, she spoke. "They said it's going to be close. Her temperature is 106."

The bottom dropped from my stomach. I sagged against the wall. "106?"

"They've attached several IVs and are administering the most potent antibiotic available." Jen's voice sounded detached, as if she were reciting dry, clinical facts—another little trick we'd learned to use over the past few months in order to survive. "They said . . ." She hesitated again. This one longer and more torturous than the first. "They said the next few hours will tell."

I didn't speak. I may have whispered a silent prayer, I don't remember. I do remember taking a long, deep breath and trying to quiet my thoughts. So this was it. After all of these months of anguish and struggle . . . it finally came down to the next few hours, to some unknown infection that had crept in almost without our knowing.

"Paul? Are you there?"

My voice came back thick and husky. "Yeah."

"What about... Have you checked on..."

"The leaf?"

She said nothing. She didn't have to. I was already standing at our daughter's window. I'd pulled up the shade several minutes earlier. It was now five in the morning and the predicted storm, the one we'd been fearing, was in full force. Shadows from the streetlight danced crazily across the backyard as the bare branches of the old maple, the one between the house and the detached garage, whipped and slapped at each other. Through sheets of water sliding down the glass, I caught a glimpse of a yellow and blackened leaf. It stood stalwart in the blowing wind, clinging to a large branch that stretched out over the garage roof. It was the last leaf on the tree. And, as it had remained throughout the fall, the winter, and now in the approaching spring, it had become the symbol of our family's hope ... and of our fears.

"It's still there," I said.

I could practically hear her relief. "How are Sammy and Heather?"

"I got them back into bed and quieted down. They're probably asleep by now." I glanced at my watch. "I don't know what's taking Jeff so long; he should already be here. Maybe I'll just pack them up and head on down to join—"

"No." Jen's voice was quiet but firm. "You know how Heather freaks in storms. If you've got them in bed, let them sleep. Just stay until Jeff shows up."

"Jen—"

"Please, Paul. It'll only be a few minutes."

I nodded. She was right. Sam and his little sister had been through enough already. They didn't need any more panicked trips to the hospital, any more fears of seeing their big sister die. No, Ally's sickness had robbed them of enough already. It had robbed us all. Besides stealing Ally's leg, her hope for the future, and her faith in God, it had also destroyed Sammy and Heather's innocence—their childhood belief that they would always be safe and secure. Practically every night now, six-year-old Heather finds some excuse to pad into our room and join us in bed. And eleven-year-old Sam? Well, his emotions are more hidden, but they are just as tattered.

I glanced back out Ally's window. "You'll let me know the slightest change?" I asked.

"Of course."

"And Jen?" I gave a quick swallow. "Let's not stop praying. Whatever we do, let's not give up now."

She gave no response.

"Jen?"

"I heard you," she said. "I'll do my best."

"Me too." I took a breath and quietly repeated. "Me too."

There was a quiet click as she hung up. I followed suit more slowly.

Now I was alone in my seventeen-year-old's bedroom. There was only the wind, the scratch of branches against the house, and the drumming rain—the perpetual, drumming rain. I'd called Jeff right after Jenny had left to follow the ambulance to the hospital. As an elder in my church and my closest friend, he and his wife were my first choice to come and stay with the kids. But the storm had obviously slowed them down—that, and making those first couple calls to start up the church prayer chain. After all, it's not every night the pastor's firstborn has to fight for her life.

I closed my eyes. If only it was that simple. The real problem was she no longer wanted to fight. I dragged my hand across my face. My forehead was wet and cold, my jaw a stubble of two day's growth.

"My God..." The groan surprised me, coming somewhere deep in my gut. When I opened my eyes I saw I was looking across the room at the top of Ally's dresser. Much of the white pine was dominated by a CD boombox. The rest was cluttered with ceramic knickknacks, makeup, bracelets, a few leftover Beanie Babies from her younger days, a candle or two, a small vase of tiny red dried flowers, and photos of friends and family—even one of me standing with my arms wrapped around her on the beach back when we'd vacationed in Florida.

Above the clutter rose her mirror. The mirror that, a half year ago, had been plastered with cutout magazine photos of models and ballerinas. Models, because my child, like most teenagers, was the victim of gaunt, media role models, who stared at her accusingly for having the slightest trace of body fat or for actually enjoying a normal meal. How many times had I seen her deprive herself, insisting that a handful of carrot sticks actually filled her up, or watched her stew in guilt that she'd given in to temptation and "binged" on a whole side of fries? (What bitter irony this would become when, during the past few months, my Ally would have given anything to *stop* losing weight and to actually gain it.)

And the pictures of the ballerinas? They'd been on the mirror because, for as long as I can remember, my little girl had wanted to be a dancer.

MEMORIES RUSHED IN. MEMORIES of four-year-old Ally in preschool, tears welling up in those big brown eyes, pleading with the after-school dance teacher to let her take ballet with the bigger kids.

"I'm sorry," the teacher explained to her in a condescending, singsong voice. "Preschool is just a little too young, isn't it? Maybe next year, when you're a big kindergartner."

I remember Ally biting her lip and trying to hold back the tears. But if there was one thing my daughter is, it's determined. Not long after the confrontation with the dance teacher came that fateful day when I was scheduled to pick her up after preschool. Jen was having a rough pregnancy with Sam so I was on transportation duty.

"Hey, Gloria," I said, as I entered the classroom.

"Hi, Pastor." Gloria, a bespectacled twenty-somethinger, had been attending my pre-marital class with her fiancé the past several months.

"How was Ally today?" I asked.

Gloria turned to me with a smile. "Still redefining the term *strong-willed.*"

"What did she do this time?"

"Actually, today, not much. Except when one of the children asked where the white in snow goes after it melts. I tried to explain that it simply evaporates, but Ally wasn't buying that for one second."

"You two had another 'discussion'?"

She chuckled. "More like a full-out debate."

"And her position was. . ."

"It seems that the white of the snow is absorbed right into the ground with the water."

"Makes sense to me," I said.

She nodded. "Then when the tree roots drink it, it's sucked up into the branches."

"And. . ."

"And when they cut down the tree and make paper out of it, well, that's where the white goes."

"Into the paper."

She nodded. I smiled, impressed, but not surprised. Even then Ally had her own type of logic. Glancing around, I asked, "So where is she?"

"Didn't your wife pick her up?"

"Not today, that's my assignment."

"Are you sure? She grabbed her lunch pail and coat and said she was going, so I just naturally figured—"

"Jen is at home; I just spoke with her."

The look on Gloria's face said it all. Without a word the two of us quickly headed out of the classroom and into the hall.

"Ally?" I called. "Ally, are you here?"

We worked to keep our voices calm. "Ally?" We moved down the hall, sticking our heads into each classroom. "Ally?" But she was nowhere to be found.

"Maybe she's outside," Gloria said. "Maybe she's waiting in the parking lot."

I frowned. "She knows better than that."

We turned and headed back down the hall, our footsteps measured but urgent. I pushed open one of the glass doors and stepped into the low-angle light of a winter afternoon.

"Ally. . ." Plumes of breath rose from my mouth. "Ally?"

"There," Gloria pointed. "Over there at the end of the building."

I turned and spotted her. She stood near the corner in the lengthening shadows, silently spying into a classroom.

"Ally?" She did not answer. I started toward her. My feet crackled across the freezing slush. "Ally, what are you doing?"

As I approached I saw that the classroom was full of ballet dancers. And, as the students went through their routines, Ally stood in the numbing cold, pointing her little feet the way they pointed their feet, bending her little knees the way they bent theirs.

I finally arrived, scooping her into my arms. "Ally!" She endured my hugs and patiently tolerated my lecture . . . while all the time keeping an eye on the activities inside the classroom.

Yes, it had become obvious, even at the tender age of four, that my little girl had found her life's calling. And so began my life as a *Dance Dad*. . .

Soon, everywhere I turned there were pink tights, black-and-white leotards, unbelievably expensive toe shoes, blistered feet, and the perpetual spinning and twirling as I tried to carry on any conversation with her.

Then there was the Nutcracker—year after year after year of . . . the Nutcracker. Don't get me wrong, I have nothing against that ballet, but how many performances can a man endure as his child moves up the ranks from playing gingerbread children, to mice, to party girls, to snowflakes, and on and on, and on some more. In fact, if it were not for portable cassette recorders, along with those little earphones you can fit into your ear with nobody noticing, as well as books on tape, I doubt I could have made it.

Now, before you label me as totally insensitive, let me point out that the use of these devices not only enabled me to endure that particular ballet but to attend it with the same enthusiasm I had the first five or six times I'd seen it. The procedure was simple; lights go down, earphones went in. When Ally came onstage, I'd hit the pause button and give her my undivided attention. When she was through, I'd hit the play button and continue my listening pleasure. And since the auditorium was always dark, no one could possibly accuse me of being rude when their own little pride and joy twittered and frittered about the stage. On the contrary, I would continue to stare ahead and pretend to enjoy myself, which I actually was (more than they could have imagined). A foolproof plan? I thought so. A win/win situation for all involved? It should have been.

Then came that fateful performance two years ago. That was the performance I had accidentally pulled the earphones out of my recorder. Naturally I didn't realize that was why I couldn't hear the cassette, which would explain why I kept cranking up the volume louder and louder until eventually John Grisham's latest thriller blasted across the auditorium full volume as a somewhat confused Sugar Plum Fairy spun herself into dizzy oblivion.

Needless to say that was the last of my book on tape days. It was also the last time Ally would let me get near an auditorium without first giving me a careful body search.

I SMILED ALMOST RUEFULLY as the memory faded. It had been so many lifetimes ago. I looked back to the dresser mirror. There were no magazine cutouts on it now. No models. No ballerinas. Now, there was only the dull film of adhesive strips where they had once been taped to the glass. Ally had disposed of the pictures long ago—back when she'd lost hope, back when she'd quit believing in God.

The thought tightened my stomach.

God. . .

What an important part He played in my life. In all of our lives. As a third-generation pastor, He was all I hoped in. All I lived for. Everything I did was to serve Him, to serve His people. Until now. . .

Because now I wasn't so sure who He was anymore.

Oh, I still believed. I'd be a fool not to. And I'd always love Him. As the Scriptures say, "Though he slay me, yet will I hope in him." But now . . . now like Sammy and little Heather, my world was no longer as safe and secure as it once was. I could no longer claim to know Him as I once had. Now, in the darkest corners of my soul I was full of doubt and fear and anger. And those emotions scared me almost as much as the prospect of losing my daughter.

I turned and glanced back out her window, catching a glimpse of the leaf and the garage directly below it, the garage we had turned into an art studio for Dad after he'd moved in with us. The garage where, after his retirement from ministry, he spent dozens of hours a week painting. He wasn't great but, like Ally, he was determined. When questioned about this new passion of his, he'd just smile and say he was trying to capture God's love on the canvas. Some of the older members of the congregation complained that he was wasting his time. "A man of such experience should never retire from ministry," they said. "He should use his skills to help mentor younger, less gifted pastors." (*Like his younger and less gifted son,* I'm sure they mentally added.) Still, Dad had been a pastor since he was eighteen. He deserved some rest.

But it wasn't exactly rest. For my father, painting had grown into an act of worship, another way of communing with the Savior he so deeply adored.

"If I could just capture a smidgen of His love," he would say. "If I could just show the love He had for us up on that cross, then I'd be content."

"So do it," a younger, fourteen-year-old Ally had challenged him one day in the studio.

"Do what?"

"Paint a picture of Jesus hanging on the cross."

I remember my father turning to her from his easel, his hazel eyes searching hers. He pushed back his thin hair and shook his head. "No, girl, it's been done a million times before."

"So what's wrong with doing it a million and one?"

He flashed her his famous, uneven smile—the one that gave him so much character. When he'd been a child, braces were unheard of, unaffordable. As an adult, he'd never had the inclination. "Remember how we used to say the words 'toy boat' over and over again?" he asked. "Do you remember?"

She nodded. "Sure."

"How we'd say them faster and faster, until we couldn't say them anymore, until they didn't have any more meaning?"

She nodded again.

"That's how it is with me. You're right, there's no greater picture of God's love than Jesus on the cross. But I've seen so many paintings of it, over and over again, that part of me has grown numb to it—not to what Jesus did, but to the paintings. There's got to be another way to capture that love. That's what I want to do, Buddy Girl. I want to capture and express that same love but in a way that's fresh and alive and powerful."

Ally looked at him, trying to understand.

He continued, "It's like when you're dancing. Do you go through the same routine, performance after performance, without thinking?"

Ally frowned. "Of course not. I've got to feel it. I've got to feel the emotion in the music and put it into my movement. Otherwise I'd be bored out of my head, and so would the audience."

"Exactly. And the same is true with my painting. I want to experience that love. I want to explore it and capture its power . . . for myself and for those who look at it."

Ally watched him, slowly starting to nod. Apparently the answer had satisfied her. I wasn't sure how, but it didn't matter. The two spent a lot of time in his studio talking like that, artist to artist—often in a language I only pretended to understand.

And it was there, in that same garage, just seven months ago, after Ally had been diagnosed with cancer, that I had my own talk with Dad. Well, actually, I really wasn't talking. More like raging . . .

"It's not fair!" I roared. "She's only seventeen. *Seventeen!*"

Dad sat quietly on his wooden stool in front of a canvas, another one of his landscapes. I didn't expect him to answer. As a pastor for fifty years, he had long ago learned the wisdom of not stepping between God and His children when punches were being thrown. Instead, he allowed me to continue venting as I stormed back and forth across the studio like a caged animal.

It was the end of July. The air inside was hot and heavy with moisture. Ten days earlier Ally had convinced her mother to take her to the doctor about a persistent ache in her left knee.

"It's just growing pains," Jennifer had assured her.

But Ally disagreed. "Mom, I'm seventeen. I quit growing back in tenth grade."

"Maybe you hurt something in dance. Maybe you just pulled a—"

"Mo-om..."

"Honey, we can't afford to go running to the doctor every time you—"

"Mo-o-omm..."

As usual, Ally's persistence paid off. Soon they visited our family physician who took some X rays of her leg. After studying the pictures he immediately made an appointment for them to visit an orthopedic surgeon, who immediately sent them to an orthopedic oncologist.

That's when we first heard the word *osteosarcoma.*

Next came what the doctors called "staging." In just a matter of hours they had performed what seemed to be every test known to man, and then some. Blood work, more X rays, CAT scans, MRI, bone scan, chest X ray, chest CTS, and finally the infamous "incisional biopsy," a procedure where they removed a section of bone near Ally's knee to examine it under a microscope. Then, finally, after five agonizing days of waiting, praying, and leaping every time the phone rang, the results from the oncologist came in:

"I'm sorry, Pastor." Dr. Lawson's voice was gentle but full of quiet resolve. "There's no easy way of saying this, but our fears are confirmed. Your daughter has bone cancer."

Back in the garage with Dad I kicked a discarded easel that had the misfortune of getting in my way. "Didn't we pray?" I demanded as I paced. "Hasn't Iris Johnson, hasn't the entire women's group been fasting and praying for us!?"

Dad said nothing. A shaft of sunlight spilled in from the doorway illuminating several canvases in glaring brightness. Some of the pictures were squares less than a foot wide. Others much larger. Some were complete, some were "works in progress," and some were works in progress that would never be complete.

Dad picked up a rag and carefully wiped the paint from his crinkled and liver-spotted hands. "What did the doctors say?" he asked. "What's their prognosis?"

I swallowed hard, staring at the floor. The multicolored streams and spatters of dried paint on the concrete blurred in my growing tears. "Three rounds of chemotherapy," I said. "Followed by surgery, then one more round of chemo."

"Surgery?" he asked.

I nodded. "First they'll kill as much cancer as possible with the chemo." I took an unsteady breath and continued. "Then they'll go in and either amputate her leg or replace parts with a prosthesis or bone from a human cadaver." I'd meant for the words to shock him, and, when I glanced up, I saw I had succeeded. The man sat speechless, his thin, white hair glowing in the sunlight.

I resumed pacing. My chest felt like I'd swallowed broken glass that pierced my lungs with every breath. "Why?" I demanded. "*Why?* Is this how He treats His servants? Is this how He rewards those who give Him their lives?"

As pastors we'd both been faced with the terrible "why" question. At hospitals, deathbeds, gravesides. And, as pastors we did our best to avoid becoming God's defense attorneys. Instead of defending Him, it was our job to simply offer His love.

Love?

I took another ragged breath. "Why would a God of love do this sort of thing? Tell me? All she's ever wanted her entire life was to be a dancer. That's all she ever dreamed of. And now to just arbitrarily chop off her leg? *Why?*"

Dad gave no answers.

I turned at him and roared. "*WHY!*"

At last he looked up. My eyes locked onto his, and he knew I wasn't backing down. "*Why?*"

He cleared his throat. "The Scriptures say—"

"I know what the Scriptures say!" I shouted. "I know *everything* the Scriptures say. But that's my little girl, not some theological treatise. She's my kid, Dad. *My* kid. And I want to know why!"

With effort he finally disengaged from my eyes and glanced about the studio. He took a deep breath but would not look back at me. "Son. . ." He hesitated, then continued. "The question is not *why,* but *how.*"

"How?"

He nodded. *"How* will God use this for His glory. *How* will He use it to demonstrate His love."

I exploded. "How do you love someone by torturing them!? How do you love a child by destroying her only dream?"

He still would not look at me, which made me all the more angry. "Answer me!" My voice rang against the wooden rafters and concrete floor. I was harsh and mean and petulant. But I was also lost and frightened. *"Answer me!"*

Finally, sadly, he shook his head. "I don't know."

I stood, feeling myself trembling with rage.

In the silence he looked about the studio, all the pictures, all the canvases. When he spoke again, it was softer, more vulnerable. "God's love . . . who can explain it? Its depth, its power."

"Isn't that supposed to be our job?" I seethed. "To explain his love?"

He thought another moment then nodded. "And I wonder if we ever really succeed . . . so awesome, so beyond our ability to comprehend, let alone communicate." He paused. "All I know is that His love is greater than any circumstance you or I will ever find ourselves in. It is greater than any disappointment we will ever face. It is greater than any suffering we will ever experience."

"And if Ally should die?" I asked.

He turned to me, blinking in surprise.

"The doctors say there's a twenty percent chance she'll not make it through the treatments. And if it metastasizes the danger rises to eighty percent. If she should die, Dad, if the cancer kills her, what then?"

He took another breath and looked to the ground. "If that should be the case, and I pray to God it isn't—"

"But if it is?" I demanded.

Slowly, he looked up, once again locking onto my eyes. "Then His love will be even greater than her death."

IN THE HALLWAY, SAMMY'S ROLLERBLADES LAY SPRAWLED BEFORE his door—another one of his valiant attempts at housekeeping. I almost smiled. On normal days his coat, schoolwork, and any other nonessentials were lucky to make it past the kitchen door, let alone all the way up the stairs and into his room. It's not that Sam is a slob, it's just—well, actually, he is a slob. Big time. And, though we still ride him about it, over the last few years we've started to grow more lenient—no longer chalking it up to disobedience, but genetics. Or as Jen was so fond of sighing, "Like father, like son..."

I stooped down to pick up the skates, but as soon as my hands touched the slick black plastic, I stopped. These once belonged to Ally. And somewhere, somewhere in the back of my closet lay a matching pair, worn only once. By me.

I remembered Jennifer's concern just a few short years ago as Ally and I had headed toward the front door...

"PAUL, DO YOU REALLY think this is such a good idea?"

"We'll be back in half an hour."

"But . . . rollerblades?"

"You know what the doctor said. I have the cholesterol level of a cheeseburger."

"With extra mayo," Dad called from the sofa.

"So the more exercise I get, the better."

"But . . . rollerblades?" she asked again.

"Why do you keep saying that?"

"'Cause you're old, Dad," Ally teased.

I threw her a mock punch, and she scooted out of reach, giggling. In less than a year the giggles would turn to eye rolling, but at eleven, the hormones hadn't hit yet, and she was still the bubbly child who was thrilled to go shopping with her father.

"Thirty-six is not old," I argued.

"It is if you break something," Jennifer observed.

As we headed out the door, I tried to calm her. "Just look upon it as a midlife crisis. Some guys go for the babes and red convertibles. I go for the—"

"Dad, they're closing in half an hour. Come on!"

"We'll be back in an hour," I assured her as I climbed into the Taurus (which is as close as any respectable pastor can come to a red convertible). Moments later we were speeding off to Wal-Mart.

When we arrived I was immediately broadsided by my eleven-year-old's logic. Not that I could blame her. Just as Sam inherited his sloppiness from me, Ally had inherited the inability to pass up any sale from her mother. Besides the *two* pairs of rollerblades (Ally had insisted she'd outgrown her pair and since they were on sale, and since I had the credit card, and since she was suddenly back to calling me "Daddy," an old ploy that works to this day . . . well, you get the picture). Besides the sale and obvious daughter/father manipulation, there were the hidden expenses . . . helmet, knee pads, elbow pads, wrist pads. The list kept growing, as did the bill.

But, I have to tell you, I was grateful for every one of those hidden expenses the next day, when my first lesson began in front of the house. . .

"No, Dad, you're just walking. You gotta skate. Push yourself off. See, like this." Ally glided effortlessly down the driveway and out into the street.

I tried to follow. The operative word is *tried*. I'd been a pretty good athlete in college and it was important that Ally know her old man had not lost his edge—even though several pounds of that edge now hung over his belt. Then there was that pastoral stigma. Gotta let them know you can love God and still be cool and hip and groovy (well, maybe not groovy, but the current slang equivalent, whatever that might be).

Those were the thoughts that filled my mind as I pushed off and headed down the driveway. And those were the thoughts that fled my brain the moment I realized we'd missed one important detail:

"How do I stop!?" I shouted as I zoomed past her.

Ally sped up and glided around me. "Like this." She dragged one foot on its side and came to a gentle stop.

It looked suicidal—I could barely stand on two skates, how was I expected to stop on one? But, as I said, I had an image to protect. Cautiously and with great trepidation, I lifted my right foot. I was just about to start dragging it when the wheels on my left hit a minuscule piece of gravel, causing me to lunge forward.

"Dad!"

The good news was I caught my balance. The bad news was that balance lasted only a second before I traded in the minuscule piece of gravel for a slightly larger army action figure Sam had left in the street. Soon I was lying face first on the pavement.

"Dad!" She raced up to me. "Are you all right?"

"Oh, sure," I said, forcing a smile (while questioning the wisdom of spending all that money on protective gear when it did nothing to alleviate multiple fractures and internal organ failure). Still, I had an image to maintain (or at least salvage), so in no time I was back on my feet heading down the street. True, I hadn't yet mastered the fine art of stopping, but I did learn to cling to every parked car along the way to keep my speed at a respectable crawl.

"Come on, Dad! Skate!" Ally shouted.

"I am!" I insisted, though my flailing arms made it look more like I was in a perpetual state of falling.

"Hey, kids, it's Pastor Newcombe," Kimberly Fuller called from her passing minivan. She honked and waved merrily.

Her kids grinned and waved merrily.

I stumbled and staggered desperately.

As I continued journeying through the neighborhood there were other, less kind observations. "Don't they got training wheels for them things?" Old Man Scaggs shouted from his porch.

"Hope your church's got good medical," his wife added.

We'd only traveled two or three blocks before all the stumbling and staggering had worn me out. Taking pity on me, Ally hollered back, "Hey, Dad, you want to stop at the 7-Eleven?"

I nodded vigorously. The store was half a block away. And, even though it was on Pinehurst, a busier street than I'd prefer,

I was thrilled with her suggestion. I was not so thrilled to realize that Pinehurst had a much steeper slope than I remembered. And, as we turned and started down that slope, I was even less thrilled to realize that there was no parking on Pinehurst. "No parking" as in there were no cars for me to grab hold of to slow down. "No parking" as in I continued picking up speed with no way to stop.

To be honest, the trip to the ER wasn't all that embarrassing—not compared to the fender bender I'd left in my wake while zipping through Pinehurst and 17th, or to the two ruts I'd left in the high-school lawn before finally crashing into their rosebushes (which, I might point out, are a lot more painful than grabbing hold of parked cars).

The good news was, the rosebushes were the only major casualties. The bad news was that for the next six weeks I couldn't show my face in town without some well-wisher asking, "Are you okay, Pastor? Are you all right?" I'm sure they were talking about my body, though the occasional smirk made me wonder if they might be referring to my mental health.

AH, LIFE IN THE fishbowl. There's no escaping it. After all, I'm a pastor and should behave like one. And if I can't count on the people to watch and secretly judge me, well, I can always count on myself. It's as if some part of me is always watching, always evaluating my every action from some distant, detached location. And it's never been harder than now, during Ally's illness. For no matter how frightened I am, no matter how my faith may falter, I always have to hold myself in check, I always have to behave appropriately.

Do I hate it? Always. Because it's not just the pressure of being on display. It's also the nagging question: How many of my actions are of a man of faith acting in faith . . . and how many of my actions are of a man of faith simply acting?

I think the worst came that evening in early August when we took Ally to the hospital for the first of her three rounds of chemotherapy. We'd been told they'd need to keep her for observation during the first round to make sure she had no allergic reaction to the drugs. Also, since they were to be given intravenously, something called a port-a-cath had to be surgically placed into her chest. And to do that meant undergoing a brief operation.

As we signed her in at the hospital, I worked hard to appear confident and relaxed. Nancy Benson, a sometimes visitor to our church, was the admitting clerk. I remember keeping the small talk going, even asking about her ailing mother. Was I concerned for her mother? Of course. Was this the time to bring it up, when my own daughter was about to begin the fight of her life? I had my doubts. Yet, we continued the chitchat as casually as if we were sitting together at some Little League baseball game. After all, I was supposed to be a pastor, a man of faith, I had no reason to be afraid.

When we finished signing in, the three of us—Jennifer, Ally, and I—headed up to Ally's room on the second floor. Even as we stepped off the elevator and passed the nurse's station, I caught myself nodding pleasant greetings to the nurses, still striving to appear confident and self-assured.

Once we arrived in Ally's room, she was her usual cool, seventeen-year-old self. "You guys don't have to hang around," she said, casually reaching for her overnight bag and starting to unpack.

In the old days I would have taken her statement at face value, but the further Ally progressed into womanhood, the more mysterious she became—at least to Sam and me. There was no doubt about it: My little girl was finally "crossing over," which meant I frequently had to take my cues from Jen to understand what she was really saying.

"I know you can manage without us," Jen answered as she absentmindedly straightened Ally's hair. "We'll just stay a few minutes, till everything gets settled."

Ally noticeably relaxed, and I had my answer. We were to stay until they kicked us out.

"Besides," I cleared my throat, trying to fit in, "if we left now, who's going to make sure you don't watch MTV?"

She gave me one of her Ally looks, something she'd been refining the past three or four years, that perfect blend of wincing disdain and suffering tolerance. A look, that if a guy's wife didn't clue him in, could make him a little insecure.

Minutes later, after she had changed into her gown, a middle-aged nurse with graying yellow hair whisked into the room. "Here we go," she cheerfully said. In her hands she held an IV needle.

"What's that?" Ally asked.

"To administer the anesthetic for the operation," the nurse said. She gave what was supposed to be a reassuring smile. "Now may I have your hand, sweetheart?"

And that's when it hit me. Instantly, my denial was stripped away. Suddenly my casualness was exposed. My daughter was dying of cancer. She was about to begin a journey in which there would be no turning back. This was the very first step.

Soon they would be pumping powerful poisons into her body. Poisons that would attack and kill the cancer killing her. Of course we'd been thoroughly briefed about the side effects of these poisons—the loss of hair, the nausea, the sores in the mouth—and we'd discussed it among ourselves, agreeing that it was the lesser of two evils. But now . . . to know that this was the beginning, the beginning of that long and torturous road. . .

But Ally, the tough one, the one who always disdained emotional sentimentality (or at least pretended to), held out her hand for the nurse to take. She didn't say a word. Nor did Jen. Nor did I.

I was able to hold off betraying my fears until the nurse took her hand, turned it over, and found a vein. That's when my eyes darted to Jen's, and hers to mine. The look of concern between mother and father only lasted a second—but it was long enough for Ally to spot. And to suddenly freeze. What little resolve she had managed to muster disappeared, immediately drained. And, as the nurse began to disinfect the back of her hand, Ally stared at me, sharing a moment of non-spoken fear that broke my heart:

Daddy, you said this was okay! Daddy, tell me what to do. Daddy, I'm scared. Pick me up, carry me away, and take me home. Tell me God's not mad at me. Tell me this isn't a punishment. Daddy, tell me He still loves me.

I saw all of that and more in my daughter's eyes. But instead of ordering the nurse to stop until we addressed these fears, instead of taking my daughter into my arms and assuring her that God was not mad and that, although it would be tough, we'd get through this, I merely gave an unspoken nod. That was it. That was all I gave my child—a nod. With the nurse standing right there, anything more would have been inappropriate.

Inappropriate? My daughter was petrified. She was about to begin the most terrifying journey of her life. She needed all the assurance I could give her. And I was concerned about being *appropriate!?* What type of father thinks like that? What type of human acts like that?

But Ally understood. Life in the fishbowl. It's not a life lived only by preachers but also by their families. Without hesitation, she allowed the nurse to insert the needle into her hand. She gave only the slightest wince as it entered.

The nurse smiled, hooked up the IV, and said something about returning in a few minutes.

Jen gave some sort of reply.

But I was too full of guilt and self-loathing to hear. It wasn't until the woman left the room that I noticed both Jennifer and Ally staring at me.

"You okay?" Jen asked.

"Dad?"

I cranked up a smile. "Yeah," I coughed slightly. "I'm fine." But the hoarseness in my voice betrayed me. "I just, uh, I need to get a drink of water."

"You're sure you're all right?" Jen repeated.

"Yeah. It's just awfully dry in here. Isn't it dry in here?"

Neither replied.

Turning toward the door I added, "I'll be right back."

I headed into the hall. The water fountain was at the far end. As I walked, the accusing thoughts grew louder. *Hypocrite! Your own daughter was crying out to you, and you didn't have the decency to help her! You're more concerned about what some nurse thinks than about the welfare of your own flesh and blood!* Part of me knew I was blowing it out of proportion, but instead of relief, that thought only added fuel to the fire. *And now you're out here thinking about yourself, about your own, self-indulgent behavior!*

I immediately recognized the Accuser's voice. Like every Christian, I'd fought it more times than I could count. But it didn't make what was being said any less true. My daughter was fighting for her life, and what was I doing? Not only playing pastor, but being caught up in some self-analytical indulgence.

No.

I slowed to a stop.

No!

Hypocrite or not, I was the father of the little girl back in that room. Self-indulgent or not, I was still a man who loved his daughter and trusted his Lord. I took a deep breath to steady myself. I wasn't sure what would happen. I wasn't sure what God had planned. But I was sure of these two things: I loved God, and I loved my daughter. And, despite my failures, despite my "pastoral performance," despite my thousand and one other weaknesses, I would stay by her side. I would fight this one with her. I would use one hand to hold onto hers and the other to hold onto God's. And I would not let go.

I turned and started back toward Ally's room.

I could not let go.

I GLANCED AT MY WATCH: 5:18. WHAT WAS KEEPING JEFF? HE should be here by now. I strode back down the hall to our bedroom. I grabbed the phone and quickly punched in his number. Time had slowed to a crawl. It took forever to ring. Another gust of wind hit the house—so hard that the entire structure shuddered. As always, I carried the mental picture of the tree outside Ally's room. More important, I carried the picture of the last leaf on that tree. It never left me, that leaf—it was always somewhere in the back of my mind. Tonight I continually saw it, imagining it fighting the wind, striving to hang on. Would it succeed? Would it last until morning? I didn't know.

I suppose all of that sounds superstitious. But, believe me, our concerns were anything but superstitious. It wasn't because of superstition that we worried, it was because of Ally. Because of the vow she'd made so many months before:

"When that leaf falls, I'm gone."

"What's that, sweetheart?"

"When the last leaf falls from that maple, I'll be dead."

To those outside the family, the words may have sounded like the idle threat of a self-pitying teen. But not for those of us who knew Ally and understood all she'd been through. Those of us familiar with her strong will knew that those words were anything but idle.

Nor were they idle to her oncologist:

"So much of the battle is won or lost in the patient's outlook," Dr. Lawson had said. "It's been an exhausting fight, and if your daughter is worn out, if she no longer has the strength or desire to continue, then I'm afraid..."

On the fourth ring Jeff's answering machine kicked in. It was Sally, his wife, complete with her perma-cheer voice. *"Hi there. This is the Brighton's. We're out; you're on. Beep.*

I thought of leaving a message but didn't. What good would it do? They knew I was waiting, and they were obviously on their way. I took another look at my watch. It had not changed in the last twenty seconds. Maybe they'd been in an accident? Maybe the storm had blocked the roads. I took a breath, forcing back my anxiety. Again I looked at my watch. Five minutes. I'd give them another five minutes, and if they didn't show up I'd call the Browers, or the VandenBosches, or, if necessary, even the Lamberts, anybody from the church to come over and watch the kids so I could get to the hospital.

Of course none of this would be a problem if Dad was still here. Watching the kids had been one of his favorite pastimes. Not only because he was their grandfather, but because it had become his not-so-hidden agenda to try and encourage them to love the arts as much as he did. I smiled sadly. I can't tell you how much money he'd spent on museum tickets, classical concerts, even Shakespeare—coaxing them, sometimes even bribing them, to come with him, in the hopes that someday, somehow, someway something might stick. And mid-August was no exception...

"THEY'RE TO CELEBRATE ALLEY'S success with her first round of chemo," he'd said, proudly displaying the tickets he'd just purchased, the ones for the touring Van Gogh art exhibit.

He was right—we did have plenty to celebrate. Despite all the horror stories we'd heard, the drugs, at least in the first round of chemotherapy, caused relatively minor side effects. However, going to a museum was not exactly the celebration any of us had envisioned. Still, despite the protests, we all (except for Jen who had the good sense to have a women's luncheon that afternoon) loaded into the car and wasted an entire Saturday afternoon at the museum.

"I don't get it," Heather said, peering up at the canvas before us.

"It's a cornfield," Dad said. He was almost whispering in awe. "It's his famous crows over a cornfield."

"Those are crows?" Sammy scoffed. "They're just blobs of black paint. I could do better than that. And if that's supposed to be corn . . . oh, brother."

"The colors are pretty," Heather, always the diplomat, said.

Dad continued to stand and stare. Finally, after several moments, he glanced at Ally. "What do you think, Buddy Girl?"

She shrugged. "Just 'cause some guy cuts off his ear, that's no reason to make a big deal about him."

Disappointment flickered across his face. I saw it. So did Ally, which explains her attempt to soften the blow. "But Heather's right, the colors are cool."

Tact, however, had never been Sammy's strong suit. "Doesn't look like a cornfield to me."

"It's not about a cornfield, moron," Ally replied in typical, older sister sensitivity. "It's about what he feels about the cornfield. Right, Grandpa?"

He shook his head, eyes still fixed on the canvas. "It's more than that. It's how he makes *us* feel about the cornfield. Look at it, guys. I mean really look at it. How does it make *you* feel? Look at those textures, those thick strokes of paint, can't you just feel his urgency, the passion in which he painted it? I'd give anything to do something like this. And the contrast of those yellow stalks against the black and blue storm clouds. Can't you feel his desperation? Don't you just ache with his hunger to connect with the eternal?"

The kids stared blankly—though the word "hunger" did stir up one emotion.

"I'm starved," Sammy complained.

Dad said nothing, continuing to gaze at the painting.

Sammy looked back at me. "Can't we get something to eat?"

Having always leaned more toward Sammy's artistic tastes, I gave him a nod and motioned for him to quietly join me. Heather spotted our communication and pulled herself from Dad's hand to follow her big brother. But not Ally. Like my father, she was now staring at the canvas, allowing it to work its power, allowing herself to be swept away by its passion.

I'll never forget the two of them standing there, so entranced. And, though part of me was a little jealous that they were touching and sharing in something I could never understand, another part of me was pleased. They were such good friends. That was good for Alley, yes, but more importantly, it was good for Dad. Because in those first few years after turning the church over to me, and later in losing Mom, he seemed to have lost himself, to have forgotten who he was ... as if he no longer had an identity.

Of course, as a brash young man, just out of seminary, I took little notice. After all, I was going to change the world. I was going to pick up where my father had left off and turn the community upside down. Little did I realize that I was the one who was to be turned upside down. I was the one who would learn, day by day, that God was not interested in big, fancy ministries, but rather that He was interested in needy individuals. Gradually, day by day I was the one who learned that the American dream of "bigger is better" did not apply to God's kingdom. He didn't need superstar pastors. He wanted obedient servants of God whose hearts were tender toward His flock. Tender, concerned hearts, that's what He was after. And the good news was, it made little difference whether those hearts were attached to feet of clay. Because there's no quicker way of spotting a man's clay than through his family. I smiled wistfully, remembering my first sermon at Dad's church...

"Ladies and gentlemen."

I'd given several talks when I was his youth pastor and attending seminary, but now here I was, delivering my first sermon as "Senior" Pastor.

"I know some of you are nervous about my stepping into Dad's shoes. But if it's any consolation, none of you are more nervous than myself."

"Wanna bet?" Dad called from the front pew beside Mom and Jen.

The congregation chuckled, and I forced a smile. But he'd already thrown off my rhythm, and I had to look back at my notes to find my place.

"He was a great man. And a great pastor."

"Sounds like you're already dead," Jeff Brighton called to my father from a few rows back.

More laughter. A little longer. Once again I grinned. Then I swallowed. My mouth had grown strangely dry. This was harder than I'd expected. I glanced at Dad, who gave me a wink of encouragement. I knew it was supposed to help, but somehow it only made me more self-conscious. Again I looked at my notes, nervously scanning them for my place.

"And a great pastor," I repeated. I cleared my throat. "I have learned much from him. And for that I am grateful." If my mouth was dry before, it was like the Sahara Desert now. I scanned the congregation. There were faces I'd known since childhood. Old Lady Niksitch, the Dressel family, Mr. and Mrs. Evans. What business did I have telling them anything? They should be the ones instructing me. Again I repeated myself. "And for that I am grateful."

My tongue stuck to the roof of my mouth. Literally. Still I forged ahead, because the only thing greater than my fear was my young male ego. "But Dad has passed his mantle on to a new generation, and with this new generation comes a new vision, a new call."

I was their pastor now. It was up to me to rally the troops, to wake them from their complacency, to take the world by storm.

"And with that call, a cry for commitment like this church has never experienced before. A cry to become the biggest and the best. For our God is not a second-rate God."

Over the years, and by His grace, most of what I said that morning has been forgotten. But I still remember enough to make me cringe:

"Now is the time for change! Now is the time to quit resting on our holier-than-thou laurels! Because now we will begin taking this city, no, this entire nation for God!"

It was hard to tell by their stoic faces if I was having any effect upon them, but I was definitely having an effect upon me. As I continued to speak I grew more and more impassioned.

"It is time to set aside old things. Old ideas and old ways of thinking must go. It is a time for a fresh new voice, a fresh new vision. And as your pastor I am ready for that challenge. I am ready to lead us into battle. For in Christ we can do all things. In Christ we can—"

"Daddy . . . icky. Daddy."

I froze mid-sentence.

"Icky-pooh."

I glanced up, unable to move. For there, toddling down the center aisle, buck naked from the waist down, was two-year-old Ally. In her hand was the dirty diaper she had just pulled off and was waving high above her head.

"Daddy, icky-pooh. . ."

Apparently someone in the nursery had made the mistake of leaving the door open, and the even bigger mistake of expecting our daughter to stay put . . . especially when she had a dirty diaper that needed changing. Well, if the nursery attendant didn't know how to fix the problem, Ally knew Daddy did. And there I was. Right up there on the platform in plain sight.

"Icky-pooh, Daddy. Icky-pooh."

Thus ended my first sermon. And the beginning of my understanding that I would not be the next great prophet of God. No, I would not become some super man of God, but a real man with real strengths, real weaknesses . . . and a real family. A man who would nurture and care for people like himself, people with real strengths and weaknesses and families. And, although that first lesson came hard, with several refresher courses to follow, I owe much of that learning to my family. Especially to my strong-willed Ally.

Because Ally did have a strong will.

When the last leaf falls, I'll be dead.

Actually, she had a will of iron. I knew that from the first few minutes she was born when I held her in the delivery room. . .

"WHAT AM I DOING wrong?" I shouted over her crying.

"Nothing." The nurse smiled as if she knew some great secret while placing my hand further under the baby's head.

"But she won't stop bawling," I shouted.

"That's just her way."

"Her way?" I shouted. "What do you mean, 'her way'?"

"I mean it takes some children longer to accept change than others."

"What does that mean?"

There was that smile again.

"What are you saying?" I repeated.

"I'm saying it's time to buckle in, Pastor. You're going to be in for one incredible ride."

The nurse couldn't have been more right. Everything about Ally was a struggle. Between Jen and me, we must have read every strong-willed child book written. It's not that Ally was unruly or disobedient, it just took a little longer to convince her that we were the ones raising her and not the other way around.

Besides the day-to-day struggles there was that ongoing stress of being in public. I'll never forget the afternoon I stood in line with her at Home Depot. She was all of eighteen months old...

"We mustn't stand in the grocery cart, sweetheart. We need to sit down."

My little bundle of energy nodded obediently and sat down. Then she immediately stood back up.

"No, sweetheart, you need to sit down."

She nodded, sat down, and stood back up.

"No, Ally. Sit down and stay down."

First came the scowl.

"Ally."

I could already see the wheels turning inside her head.

"Ally, sit down."

Next her bottom lip protruded.

"Ally..." I gently took her shoulders and tried to force her down. But at eighteen months the girl already had powerful dancer legs, and it was not as easy as I'd thought.

"Ally ... Ally, sit."

By now our dueling egos had attracted the attention of others standing in line ... which meant there was no longer any room for negotiation. I had to let her (and my fellow shoppers) know who was boss. "Ally, sit."

Using more force than I wanted, I finally managed to make her sit down. She had no option. However, she did have the option of letting me know her displeasure. And after two or three minutes of voicing that displeasure (at the top of her lungs), my fellow shoppers began showing signs of the stress. Some leaned toward me, offering such helpful suggestions as:

—"Know what they say, 'Spare the rod and spoil the child.'"

—"My two-year-old nephew is on Ritalin, and it's done him wonders."

—"You might want to check out Aisle Three—the duct tape is on sale."

Embarrassing? Of course. It made no difference that the books said this was normal and a sure sign of her potential as a leader of the future. Forget the future, forget leadership, back then I just wanted to survive.

Then there were the other times...

LIKE THE DANCE RECITAL when she was five years old. It was just before Easter and every human fit to be a parent had their cameras up and videotapes rolling as the class flittered about the stage in what was supposed to be a carefully choreographed number. Although, to the untrained eye it looked like random chaos, that didn't stop the mandatory oohs and aahs from the audience.

And then it happened. Little Isabel, Ally's best friend, suddenly froze. The rest of the class continued to jump and turn and flap their arms, but little Isabel stopped and stood in rigid fear. Unsure where to go and looking very much like a deer caught in headlights, she stared out at the audience, tears of fright beginning to spill onto her cheeks.

No one was sure what to do. Turn off the music? Stop the performance? A possibility, but the others had worked so hard.

Then Ally saw her. Immediately, she broke from the pack and in front of the entire audience walked across the stage to join her little friend. Without a word, she gently reached out and took Isabel's hand. Then she gently led her across the stage to where she should be and returned to her own position . . . all this as the dance continued.

At no time in my life have I been more proud of my daughter. Nor was there a more defining moment of how her iron will, when properly directed, could touch and change the world. That is the person my Ally is. That is the woman she will someday become.

IT'S MEMORIES LIKE THOSE that have pulled me through the more difficult times. Especially when we entered the turbulent and insane era known as (insert scary music here) "The Teenage Years."

Now, initially I had the upper hand. After all, I'd been a youth pastor, I knew all the tricks, and more importantly she knew I wasn't afraid to use them.

Having problems with your daughter giving you too much lip as you drop her off in front of the middle school? I found that the best cure is to roll down your window and shout after her, "Oh, honey, did you bring your extra pair of Little Mermaid underwear in case you have an accident?"

Cruel? If that's what you're thinking, then it's obvious you've never had a teenager. Those of us with experience know we need all the tools we can get. Anything goes . . . as long as it doesn't leave visible scars and you don't have to pay for too many therapy sessions.

Having a problem with arguments that lead to shouting and the slamming of her bedroom door? Nothing that a screwdriver and a place to store the door won't fix.

And the perpetual war over what is and is not acceptable music? Some might consider taking away her CDs. But this is the obvious sign of an amateur—after all, there's nothing to stop her from borrowing the contraband from friends and playing it very low when the rest of us are in bed. I found a more effective cure was to replace the CD player with the record player stored up in the attic, while leaving nothing in the house but Grandpa's old classical albums.

Yes, these tricks of the trade pulled us through those first few years of adolescence. There was also the more serious advice from acclaimed experts who said that the person your teenager is outside your house is the person they will be when they become adults.

What a relief it was to know that. Because as soon as Ally stepped outside our walls and interacted with others, she instantly ceased being Princess Me-a (the most selfish creature in the universe), and actually became a loving, caring, sensitive human being. It was probably that advice, more than any other, that gave us the courage to carry on in the hope that we were not raising some self-centered sociopath.

But that didn't stop the comments from others. Most congregations have them, that handful of individuals who are privy to all of God's spiritual secrets. Those who have, through one or two Scriptures, found the shortcut to all spiritual maturity that the rest of us have missed. Our church was no exception...

"I THINK WE'VE FINALLY found it, Pastor."

"It?" I asked, leaning back in my office chair. I already knew where the conversation was going, but I also knew I had to play along.

"Yes, the spirit that has been plaguing our congregation all these months."

For the most part I liked Mrs. Frampton and her husband (though I think he and I had exchanged a grand total of two sentences since they'd joined the congregation ten months earlier). They were an older couple with hearts that seemed committed to the Lord. That was the upside. The downside was that they saw a demon behind every unexplained event, and the phrase "just believe" had become their solution to every problem.

Don't get me wrong. I believe both principles are valid. As a short-term missionary in college, I'd seen more demonic activity than most ... and I'd seen the power of faith overcome insurmountable odds. But when misapplied, I've also seen these two principles tear a congregation apart. And since we'd been hitting some heavy budgetary problems lately and since there had been a recent decline in attendance ... well, the Framptons had found all the excuses they needed to go on the prowl.

At first they were sure it was Sean Martin, our worship leader. After all, he'd been bringing in all those contemporary songs for the congregation to sing. After they'd finally been convinced that he wasn't the cause, they felt it was those worldly teens our youth group had started inviting to church. When that didn't pan out, they finally discovered the real source...

"It's your daughter, Pastor. She's the reason for the dropping attendance."

"I see," I coughed slightly, doing my best to keep my irritation in check.

"She has a spirit of rebellion that's oppressing the congregation."

Mr. Frampton sat beside his wife, nodding.

I threw a nervous glance toward the adjoining office where Ally was doing her homework. As a junior in high school, she often stopped by after school to catch a ride home. Needless to say, I hoped the paper-thin walls were blocking out the conversation.

I cleared my throat and asked, "And the reason you believe this?"

Mrs. Frampton snorted. "Well, just look at her behavior, Pastor. She's got demon possession written all over her."

Mr. Frampton nodded.

"I see..." By the grace of God I had managed to hide my anger. As I said, these were loving, concerned people—perhaps not as balanced as I'd like, but good people. Still, there was the other problem. How much longer could the congregation endure such self-appointed witch-hunts without starting to crack? Already several members were voicing their concern and feeling the strain. It had been a prickly problem for months, and one that I still hadn't a clue how to solve.

"Mrs. Frampton," I said in a measured tone. "I appreciate your concern. And admittedly Ally does have some strong opinions—"

"Exactly," Mrs. Frampton interrupted.

Mr. Frampton nodded.

"—and it's true we've been working with her in areas of obedience—"

"Precisely," she agreed.

Mr. Frampton nodded.

"But to attribute this to any type of demonic activity ... well, I'm just not—"

We were interrupted by an ear-splitting shriek from the next room.

"What's that?" Mrs. Frampton cried.

I was up and out of my seat. "I don't know." I threw open the door. There was Ally in the chair behind her desk, her entire body writhing, her head tossing back and forth. Her cry now giving way to whimpering groans.

"Ally!" I raced to her side. "Ally, what's wrong?"

More writhing and groaning.

"Ally!"

"Step aside, Pastor." Mrs. Frampton placed a hand on my shoulder.

I looked up, confused, as Ally continued to thrash about. "What?"

"We've seen this sort of thing before," Mrs. Frampton explained. "Please, we know what to do." She gently pulled me back.

"But—"

"It's okay, we're experts."

I turned to Mr. Frampton, who nodded. Dazed and uncomprehending, I stepped aside as Mrs. Frampton raised her hand high above my moaning daughter. What was she doing? What was going on?

"Demon!" Mrs. Frampton's voice filled the tiny office.

Ally continued to toss back and forth.

"Demon, by all that is good and holy ... *I command you to leave!"*

Ally continued to writhe.

I moved in. "Look, I don't know what's going on, but—"

Mr. Frampton held out his arm, blocking my path.

"Now!" Mrs. Frampton cried. "I command you to leave her ... *now!"*

Suddenly Ally's body arched. Her head flew back, and she let out an deep, unearthly scream.

I stood dumbfounded.

The cry continued a good ten seconds before the last of her breath was exhaled. When it had finally finished, Mrs. Frampton turned to me. With a smile, she whispered, "She'll be okay now."

"What?" I asked.

"It's gone, Pastor. She'll be all right now. Everything will be all right."

I watched, still confused, as Mrs. Frampton stooped down to speak with Ally, brushing back her hair, sharing quiet words of comfort and encouragement.

I finally found my voice. "Ally? Are you all right? What's going on, what happened?"

She looked up at me with a weak, exhausted smile. "I'm okay now, Daddy," she sighed. "I'm all right."

"But—"

"Really. Everything's fine." Turning to the Framptons, she whispered, "Thank you." Taking both of their hands and squeezing them, she repeated, "Thank you so very much."

The couple nodded and rose. It wasn't until the good-byes were finally exchanged and they headed out the door that the realization began to sink in.

"Well, now," Ally said, rising from the chair and casually straightening her blouse. "That should take care of that."

"What?" I said, my mouth sagging open as she started collecting her books. "What just happened?" I asked. "What did you do?"

"I believe it was a scene from *The Exorcist*—although you've never let me watch it."

"Ally..."

"What'd you think of the head rolling? Nice touch, wasn't it?"

"Ally Newcombe."

By now she had grabbed her jacket and was moving toward the door. "Dad, you know they wouldn't let up until they got their way. And you told me yourself how they could hurt the church."

"You mean to tell me..."

She smiled.

"You mean you just..."

She shrugged. "They wanted a demon, so I gave them a demon. Now can we go home? I'm starved."

Despite the poor taste she'd demonstrated, I had to admit, the problem of associating demon possession with our low attendance never again resurfaced. In one rather bad Linda Blair impression, Ally had solved a dilemma I couldn't begin to touch, and saved the church from some very serious problems. Amazing.

But that wasn't my last surprise regarding the Framptons. As I said, though I disagreed with their approach, I did appreciate their commitment. And it was at the end of August, just before Ally began her second round of chemo, that I once again had the opportunity to experience it.

I'd been working late on a Friday night. The final word was that we were going to have to cut back our budget by twelve to fifteen percent. I'd been in the office all afternoon trying to make the numbers work, but with little success. And by eight o'clock, the figures had become such a blur that I knew I had to call it quits and start again tomorrow.

That's when I heard a muffled voice. But that wasn't possible—the church had been locked for hours. There it was again. I reached for my desk lamp and silently snapped it off. Had someone broken in? In a larger community I might have grabbed the phone and called the police, but not here. Here, everybody knew everybody, or at least knew somebody that knew everybody. No. Chances were it was just some kids, maybe some wanna-be vandals, I could scare off by inviting to church.

I rose from my desk and quietly opened the office door, which looked out into the darkened sanctuary. There it was again. No, it wasn't a voice, it was a sob.

"Who's there?" I called.

The sound immediately stopped.

"Hello?"

No response. I reached over to the switches on the wall and turned them on. Suddenly the sanctuary was bathed in light. At first I saw nothing, then I spotted it, just above the top of the second pew. A head.

"Who's there?" I repeated.

The head looked up, and I recognized him. "Mr. Frampton?" I stepped further into the sanctuary.

He rose stiffly from his knees to greet me. "Pastor."

"What are you doing here?" As I approached I spotted a pillow on the floor near his feet. Then a thermos. "Are you all right?"

He nodded a little self-consciously.

"But why . . . I mean, it's almost eight o'clock."

"I come to pray."

"To pray?"

He nodded. I waited for more. With some difficulty he continued. "On Friday nights Doris and I, sometimes together, sometimes just one of us, we come here to pray."

I stood, staring, trying to think of a response. "How . . . how did you get in?"

He smiled, revealing his chipped front tooth. "I'm a locksmith, remember?"

I glanced down at the pillow.

"With my arthritis," he explained, "after a few hours, sometimes the floor gets a little hard."

I blinked. "Hours?"

He motioned toward his thermos. "That's why Doris fixes me the coffee."

I continued to stare, trying to absorb what I was hearing. "How long," I finally asked, "how long do you pray?"

"Depends on the need." He gave a shrug. "But since the devil's been attacking your daughter with sickness . . . usually till two or three."

"Two or three o'clock in the morning?" I asked.

"I used to go longer, but I'm not quite so young anymore."

I nodded, fighting back the emotion swelling in my chest. "Well, can I get you anything . . . I mean, would you like some company or anything?"

He broke into another grin. "No, Pastor, you go on home to your family."

"What about you? What about *your* family?"

"My kids are grown, you know that."

"Well, yes, but, I mean. . ." I struggled for the words.

"You are my family, Pastor. This congregation. . ." He paused to look about the sanctuary. "We're all God's family, ain't we."

I felt my eyes burning with moisture.

He looked back at me, his grin broadening. "You go on home, Pastor."

Without warning I reached out and hugged him. Perhaps the embrace was a bit longer than normal, and perhaps he understood why. I couldn't be sure. But I was sure of one thing. Any problems I might have had with this couple, any doubts I had about their theology were put to rest that evening. Because despite all that I'd studied and taught on Christian love, I realized I had a whole lot more to learn. More importantly, I realized who I could learn it from.

DAD'S SUGGESTION THAT WE SHOULD CELEBRATE ALLY'S SUCcessful first round of chemo had been brilliant. Because, frankly, at the end of August when she began the second of her three rounds, the results were anything but encouraging. For starters, her senior year was about to begin. This should have been the greatest time of her life—the height of youth's success mixed with the breathless anticipation of adulthood.

Instead, it was the beginning of our field trip through hell.

The doctors had been satisfied with the first round. They'd found the right combination of drugs, and there had been no allergic reaction. But three weeks later, when she began her second round, the chemicals hit hard. We'd been warned that something like this might happen, but the first round had been such a breeze that we were completely unprepared for the results of the second.

First came her lack of appetite. With Ally's pencil-thin, dancer's body, every pound she lost was a concern. And she lost several. Still, she wasn't about to give up the fight. With that iron will of hers, she forced down bite after bite of food, though the nausea always made it a gamble if it would stay down.

Then came her change in tastes . . .

"What's that smell?" I asked, coming into the kitchen early one morning.

Jennifer looked up from the oven, wiping a damp tendril of hair from her face. It was obvious she'd been up several hours. "Fudge cake with hot caramel sauce," she answered.

"For breakfast?"

Jen nodded. "She had a hard night."

I watched a moment before I continued. "I don't remember you coming to bed." She gave no answer which, of course, was the answer. "You stayed up with her again, didn't you?"

"She had a hard night."

"Jen, that's three nights this week. When's the last time you slept?"

She ignored me and checked the sauce in the pan. "I don't know why I didn't think of this earlier. This is just what she needs."

"Jen..."

She didn't answer, being careful to keep her back to me. As I sat there in the silence, watching my wife hover over the stove, a wave of admiration washed over me. It was as if I saw her beauty for the very first time. Don't get me wrong—she was no movie star, particularly in her sweats and baggy shirt. But there was a beauty there that no movie star could come close to, an inner strength that I'd always known was there but that I'd been taking for granted. Over the years this woman had endured so much—raising three kids, putting up with the non-sense from church from being a pastor's wife, from being *my* wife. And now this. I'd never had a hero before, but as I sat there watching this second-generation Italian working over the stove with her disheveled hair and baggy sweats, I realized that she was as close to one as I would ever find. I may have been the head honcho of a church, a leader in our community, but she was the mortar, the invisible glue that held us, that held *me* together. And if there was ever any doubt about where Ally got her strength, that morning, as I watched, I had my answer.

Unfortunately, Ally was not quite as appreciative. When she entered the kitchen and spotted the cake she was enthusiastic enough, and she certainly tore into it . . . but it had no sooner entered her mouth than she spat it out into the bowl. "What did you do to it?" she cried.

"What do you mean?" Jen asked.

"It tastes like manure."

"Ally!" I scolded.

"It's horrible!" She shoved the bowl away.

"Ally—"

"Taste it yourself."

"Ally."

"Taste it!"

"All right, I will." I grabbed a spoon and took a bite. "It tastes delicious," I said.

Her eyes shot to me.

"It does," I argued. "It's the best your mother ever made." I pushed the bowl back toward her. "Now I suggest you apologize to her and start eating."

"Dad. . ."

"Eat," I ordered.

"But . . . it's all bitter. It tastes like—"

"It tastes great, and you'll eat every bite!"

Suddenly, Ally's eyes welled with tears. And before I could respond, she rose from the table and headed for the stairs.

"Ally."

She picked up her pace.

"Ally, you come back here!"

"Paul," Jen interrupted, "it's okay, she doesn't have to—"

"Your mother has been working all morning for . . . Ally!"

But Ally didn't come back. Later we learned that the chemo had destroyed another part of her life—her ability to taste. Sweets became bitter, meat smelled horrific, and anything that so much as touched metal tasted metallic.

But that little change to her body was nothing compared to the big one. It was nothing compared to her loss of hair. . .

AGAIN WE THOUGHT WE'D dodged the bullet when, after the first round of chemo, it had remained. The thick copper waves that fell to her shoulders had always been one of Ally's greatest attributes (and my only contribution to her beauty). Everyone made a fuss over it when she was a child and, as with any adolescent whose identity is wrapped up in appearance, it was her crowning glory. Surely God wouldn't take that from her. With all that she'd been through, surely He would grant her that one bit of grace. At least that's what we prayed.

But one morning, after beginning the second round of chemotherapy, she found clumps of the gorgeous locks lying on her pillow.

"God. Please, no. . ."

I heard the cry from our room and quickly raced to hers. She was sitting on the bed, holding the tufts in her hands, clutching them to her face. "Please," she moaned, ". . . please . . . no . . ."

Immediately I was at her side, wrapping my arms around her.

"No," she whimpered, "please, no. . ." They were pathetic pleas. Pleas to a heaven that was growing more and more deaf. I felt her body shudder against mine, the dampness of tears soaking into my shirt. "Please," she kept repeating. "Please. . ."

Tears spilled onto my own cheeks. My throat tightened until I could barely breathe.

"Please. . ."

Jen arrived in the doorway, and I motioned for her to join us. She moved in, sitting at Ally's other side, sharing in the embrace until suddenly Ally shouted, "No!" But the shout wasn't directed at Jen. It was directed at me. She pulled from my arms then threw herself at me with clenched fists. "No!"

"Al—"

She began hitting me, pounding on me. "No! No! No!"

I tried to pull her in, partially to defend myself, partially to hold her.

"No! No!"

She held me off for as long as she could, hitting and punching. "I hate you!" She screamed. "I hate you! I hate you!"

Finally, I managed to wrap my arms around hers, pinning them to her side. "It's okay," I whispered.

"I hate you! I hate you!"

"It's okay."

"I hate you!"

"It's okay, I understand... I understand..."

And I did understand. It wasn't me she was raging at. It was Who I represented. It was the insensitive God I served. That's who she was beating upon and screaming at and hating.

Jen tried to pull her away, but I shook my head, letting the child rage and scream until finally, chest heaving for air, she collapsed, broken, into my arms. And there she remained, only an occasional sob escaping as her body continued to shudder. How long we stayed like that, I don't remember. But the memory will never fade.

Yet, despite His silence and the feeling of abandonment, there was always something, some small embrace of His that made it clear we were not alone, that He had not entirely deserted us. And that day was no exception. This time His hug came in the form of a little sister...

ALLY WAS SITTING STOICALLY that afternoon on the kitchen chair as Jen cut her hair, the shining locks falling onto the towel, then rolling and tumbling to the floor. No one was sure how much hair she would lose, but by shortening it into a bob we could disguise the humiliation a bit longer. It was excruciating for me to watch Ally sit there so emotionless. I would have given anything to see her cry again. But now there was nothing. Just numb, angry resolve.

About halfway through the ordeal, little Heather came into the room.

"What you got there, pest?" Ally asked quietly.

"Nothing," Heather shrugged, "just Molly."

Molly was the name of the American Girl doll we'd bought Heather for her birthday. It was her greatest treasure, and she carried it everywhere she went—even into the shower until we caught her. But there was something different about Molly that afternoon, and Ally was the first to spot it.

"What did you do to her?" Ally asked.

"Nothing. Just. . ."

"Come here, let me see."

Heather approached tentatively, then slowly held out her doll. Instead of the long dark hair she'd always had, Molly now sported a bob of her own. A ragged, chopped bob.

"She wanted a haircut, too," Heather said, forcing a smile. And as we all stared in silent awe, little Heather bravely presented big sister with her prized possession. "She said she wants to stay with you until you feel better."

Yes, God finds ways to speak even in His silence. And that afternoon, watching little Heather give up her greatest treasure, I knew that God was doing greater and grander things than I could have ever imagined.

UNFORTUNATELY, ALLY SELDOM SAW it that way. Instead, as the disease progressed, her resentment and anger continued to grow. *I hate you, I hate you!* At the time, her words were simply an outburst of an emotional teenager. But as those last days of August slipped into September, the words took on a more frightening truth. Oh, she would still let me talk with her. From time to time I could even get a hug out of her. But a barrier had started to grow between Ally and me. More sadly, it was growing between Ally and God.

Yet, not so strangely, there was one person who seemed able to bridge that barrier. Her grandfather. Almost always the man had the right thing to say...

"When you lose as much hair as me, then you can complain," he'd tease. Or, "Listen, bald is supposed to be sexy, at least that's what all the women tell me." Then there was his ongoing offer: "Look, if you're really concerned, I've got that old toupee I never wear. It's great, it'll make you look just like Burt Reynolds."

Maybe it was the age difference. Maybe it was their mutual respect as artists. I don't know, but somehow Dad was able to get away with things I couldn't. Sometimes it was a talk, sometimes a look, sometimes just getting to hang out with her.

I'll never forget climbing out of the car late one afternoon and practically feeling the asphalt throb with music from our garage. What on earth ... I quickly strode toward the side door, while glancing back toward the street, grateful that our neighbors hadn't yet called the cops ... or the National Guard. I opened the door and felt the air pounding with rap or hip-hop or whatever kind of music it was. And not far away, leaning on the back of a chair, surrounded by what we respectfully referred to as Dad's "works in progress" sat Ally. Her eyes were closed, and she was swaying slightly to the music. Directly beside her, sitting on his painting stool, was Dad. His eyes were also closed. Unlike Ally, he didn't appear nearly as enraptured, though the wincing frown on his face indicated deep concentration and a valiant attempt to appreciate what he was hearing ... either that or he was in pain from ruptured eardrums.

I closed the door, not wanting to intrude, and strolled across the open walkway toward the house. Dad may or may not paint his great work of art, I found myself thinking, but he was definitely helping shape another masterpiece ... his granddaughter.

"WHY DOES EVERYBODY ALWAYS treat me so different?" Ally complained one afternoon when I broke up a squirt gun fight between her and Sam in the kitchen. They were getting too rowdy and in her weakened condition during the second round of chemo I didn't want her to get hurt. "You treat me like I'm some sort of crystal that's going to break."

"We've just got to be careful until—"

"I'm tired of being careful! I want to be treated like everyone else!"

"Come on, Ally. Be reasonable."

"I'm tired of being treated like some baby!"

"Ally—"

"I want to be treated like—"

That was all she got out before Grandpa, who was standing at the sink, pulled the flex head faucet out of its holder and squirted her.

"AUGH!" she screamed, holding out her hand. "What are you doing?"

The response only encouraged him to fire off another volley.

"Grandpa!"

And another.

But the initial shock quickly passed. Now it was time for retaliation. Grabbing a glass, she raced to the refrigerator and quickly filled it with ice water from the door's dispenser.

"Ally. . . ," I warned.

She got him dead center in the face with the cold water . . . as he continued firing the hose at her.

"Ally . . . Dad!"

But the battle had begun. Soon water was flying and splashing everywhere—on the floor, on the counter, across the cupboards, as glass after glass was dumped on Grandpa, as Grandpa continued to hose her down. Unfortunately, neither had the greatest sense of accuracy and by accident or design Sam and I were soon dragged into the fight. Now everyone was going at it—shouting and screaming, ducking and dodging, splashing and soaking.

"Paul . . . Dad!" Jen raced in from the living room with Heather. "What are you doing?! Look what you're doing to my—"

That's when Ally dumped the ice water on her. Jen shrieked at the coldness but had no time to get angry as Dad immediately followed up by dousing her with the kitchen faucet. It took a moment, but once she got her bearings, Jen came back at them with equal fury, grabbing her own glass and filling it. Even little Heather got into the act. And what had once been a battle soon became an all-out war, everyone fighting for themselves, yelling, attacking, protesting in shrieks and screams. It was exactly what we needed—relief from the walking-on-eggshell tension we had endured for so many weeks. And when we had finally finished, dripping, soaked to the skin, standing in pools of water, giggling like schoolchildren, our family was closer than we had been in a long, long time.

If only it could have lasted. . .

5

THE HOUSE GAVE ANOTHER SHUDDER FROM THE WIND. I LOOKED up, startled, then glanced at my watch: 5:25! Jeff and Sally should have been here by now. Well, regardless of what was holding them up, it was time to go to Plan B. I headed out of our bedroom and into the hallway. Jen had a list of the congregation and their phone numbers downstairs in the kitchen drawer. Any one of them would be willing to come over and watch the kids so I could get to the hospital. If not, well, I would bundle Sam and Heather up and take them to the hospital.

I passed Ally's room, slowing to look out her window for the leaf. As always, I felt guilty for being so superstitious, but it didn't stop me from looking—or from feeling a surge of relief when I spotted a glimpse of it through the incessant wind and throbbing rain. Because of its position behind a gnarled, unruly branch, it could only be seen from her window. Over the months I must have looked for it a thousand times from other vantage points, both inside the house and out, with no success. But that was okay. It made it all the more special. All the more reason for it to be her leaf.

I had barely turned back to the hallway before I was hit with another memory...

"PLEASE, DON'T MAKE ME go," Ally had begged from this very room. *"Please."*

"Sweetheart," Jen tried her best to reason. "We've cleared it with the school, all the teachers understand. You can wear your hat the whole time, no one's going to make you take it off."

"But everyone will know."

It was September and the first day of Ally's senior year. Well, it was supposed to be her first day. Unfortunately by now much of her hair had fallen out, leaving large bald spots with uneven patches scattered throughout. Uneven patches that Ally had insisted be shaved off.

At one point we'd discussed buying her a wig, or making one out of her own hair, but that was not my daughter's style. She was going to be who she was regardless of what she looked like. Or so she said. But that first morning, what had sounded so noble in theory had became a nightmare in reality.

"Please," she pleaded. "Tell them I'm sick. I'll ask Isabel to get my assignments, and I can—"

"Ally," I tried to sound firm, though for the most part I was on her side. How could any teenage girl survive such humiliation. "We've already agreed," I argued. "We discussed it and this was your decision."

"I know, but—"

"Honey," Jen said. "The hat's really cute. You really look darling."

Ally moaned with typical drama. *"Darling?* Who wants to look *darling?"*

I tried again. "Listen, I know this is going to be hard, but you just can't—"

"Mom!" Sam hollered from downstairs. "Somebody's at the back door!"

"Tell them to wait a minute," Jen called back.

"But it's Ryan," he shouted.

Ally's eyes widened in fear. "Oh my gosh, Ryan."

Ryan Crenshaw was her "sort of boyfriend." "Sort of" in that neither Jen nor I were big fans of dating, so we always insisted they go in groups with other kids. And "boyfriend" in that he was inside my refrigerator more frequently than me.

"Please, don't make me see him," Ally whispered.

"Should I let him in?" Sam shouted.

"Just a minute!" Jen called.

"Please...," Ally begged. Any dramatics she'd been using were gone. This was panic. Sheer, unadulterated panic.

"Ally..."

"Mom?" Sam shouted. "Mom!"

"Just a minute," she called again.

"I'll go down and stall him," I said, turning for the stairs.

"Please, Dad," Ally pleaded. "Mom, please don't make me go..."

"Ally, sweetheart..."

The two continued their negotiations as I headed down the stairs and moved toward the kitchen door. When I arrived, I placed my hand on the knob and took a moment to crank up my pleasantries. After all, I was a pastor, everything was under control. But when I finally opened the door even I wasn't prepared for what greeted me. Because there on the porch stood Ally's two best friends—Ryan, a gangly six-footer of mostly arms and legs, and Isabel, her best friend from dance class. Both of them sporting freshly shaved heads as bald as any billiard ball.

BUT THAT WAS ONLY the beginning of September's surprises. Soon we were hit with a blow that left everyone staggering...

"What do you mean, 'metastasized'?" I demanded. I knew the news was bad; why else would Dr. Lawson have called me down to her office in the middle of a Saturday afternoon? Jennifer was off helping at a missions conference, so I was on my own. I'd already braced myself for the worst, but I still needed to hear the doctor say the words.

"It means the cancer has spread."

I blinked but held her gaze. "Spread? To where? Further up her leg?"

The woman shook her head. "No. It's spread into Ally's lungs."

"Her lungs?" I almost laughed. "How could it spread to her lungs? We're talking bone cancer. Besides, it's way down in her knee. How could it move to her lungs?"

Dr. Lawson's voice was gentle, but gravely earnest. "If osteosarcoma metastasizes, ninety to ninety-five percent of the time it's to the lungs."

I sat a moment as the news sifted from my ears into my mind and finally down into my gut. "So what do we do now?" I asked. "Move up the operation? Get the cancer out before it spreads any further?"

"I wish it were that simple."

"What do you mean? Hasn't that been the plan all along? Kill the cancer with chemotherapy, then go in and remove the affected bone?"

"Yes, but—"

"So we just go in earlier, right?"

The doctor removed her glasses and rubbed her eyes.

"Isn't that right?" I repeated. "Isn't that what we've always said?"

She replaced her glasses. "Yes."

"Then—"

"You're forgetting the chemotherapy. It's too soon, her blood count is too low."

"Wait a minute. Are you saying that the very thing that was to prepare her for the operation is now preventing it?"

"Not exactly. . ."

"Well, which is it, Doctor?"

"If you let me explain—"

"I *am* letting you explain, but you're not making sense. Are you or are you not saying that all these drugs we've been pumping into her body are now making the operation impossible?"

"I'm saying that an operation at this particular moment in time would not be a good idea."

"So when is the 'particular moment in time,' Doctor? After it takes over her lungs? After it kills her! You're supposed to be the expert here! Tell me! When? What are our options?!"

The doctor waited patiently as I struggled to regain my composure. When she was certain I was back in control she tried again. "The purpose of the chemotherapy is to kill as much of the cancer as possible so that when we go in and remove the leg there's a better chance the disease is gone."

I nodded.

"But, as you know, the chemo also knocks out much of her immune system. At this particular moment her blood count is still too low. We need to wait. To operate now would be far too dangerous."

"Dangerous?"

"It could prove fatal."

The words sat cold and heavy on my chest. When I trusted my voice I asked, "But if we wait, the cancer will spread."

The doctor said nothing. She didn't have to. I saw the answer in her eyes.

"So how long?" I asked.

"Before we can operate?"

I nodded.

"Three weeks, minimum. Maybe a month."

"Three weeks?"

"Maybe longer. It's really up to Ally and her immune system."

"And if we wait too long?"

Once again I was met by silence.

I looked down at my hands. They were a stranger's hands—old, coarse, beginning to look like my dad's. Another question was forming, bubbling up in my mind. I tried to push it aside, but it just kept coming. No matter what I did it kept rising to the surface. Finally, I looked up. "Doctor, when we started all this we agreed that you would always be candid with us."

She gave a single nod.

"At the beginning, you said Ally's chances of survival were eighty percent. Now with it metastasized and this low blood count problem..." I swallowed and continued. "Now with these other complications, what would you say . . . what are her chances now? I'm sure you told us once, but I've forgotten."

"You're a firm believer in prayer, aren't you, Pastor?"

"Yes."

"Then I would pray hard. I would pray very hard."

I nodded. "But the chances. Putting aside prayer, what would you say the percentage is now?" I looked up and held her eyes. She knew I was not backing down until I got my answer. "What are my daughter's chances?"

"With the metastasizing and having to wait. . ." She cleared her throat. "And barring any other unforeseen circum—"

"Her chances, Doctor. What are my daughter's chances of survival?"

Her answer was soft, but unflinching. "About twenty percent."

I WAS HEADING TOWARD THE KITCHEN TO START CALLING CHURCH members when the phone rang. I darted into the room without bothering to snap on the light and scooped up the receiver. "Hello, Jeff? Hello?"

"Paul."

"Where are you? What's going on?"

"Both the 205 and Kelly Way are blocked with downed trees. We're taking the back way to your place."

"Listen," I glanced at my watch though I couldn't see it. "I'll go ahead and pack up the kids and head out to the hospital. Meet me there."

"Give us ten more minutes."

I turned to the microwave. Its digital clock glowed a blue-green 5:26. The ambulance had left over thirty minutes earlier. "Jeff, I don't think—"

"Ten minutes. If we don't hit any more snags, we'll be there in ten minutes, tops."

"But what if—"

"I've got my cell phone. If we run into any more trouble I'll give you a call."

I hesitated, unsure how to respond.

"I promise. Just sit tight, Pastor. Ten minutes, and we'll be there. Any news on Ally?"

"Jen called. Said her temp's up to 106. They're pumping all kinds of antibiotics into her. They said..." I took a breath and glanced out the window at the blowing branches. "It's going to be close, Jeff."

He paused a moment. Finally, he spoke. "Just keep praying, Paul. We're on our way."

I nodded, lowered the phone, and slowly hung up. Shadows from the street lamp flickered about the countertop in front of me. I looked up to see them dancing across the cabinets and the refrigerator. Rain pelted the window in uneven surges. I was lost, unsure what to do, where to go. I started to move, but where, I wasn't certain. I found myself at the table and pulled out a chair. It gave a dull squeak as I dragged it across the linoleum. I eased myself down and glanced at the microwave clock.

It still read 5:26.

Once again my mind drifted . . .

AFTER MY MEETING WITH the doctor, Jen and I broke the news to Ally regarding the cancer's spread and the postponement of her operation. But instead of tears, instead of anger and outrage, she remained strangely quiet. Except for her eyes. I could see those deep, dark pools beginning to think, to test, to draw conclusions. And, as I watched, I saw a steely resolve begin to grow. I knew it could go either way—the news could motivate her iron determination to trust in God regardless of the situation, regardless of the odds.

Or, it could push her the other direction, away from Him.

Two hours later I had my answer. She was in bed resting, and Dad was up in her room, participating in another one of their "discussions." As the alien parent who never understood anything, I had resigned myself to sitting on the hallway floor by her door, out of sight but within easy listening distance. I had not come to spy, but to listen and learn.

"Don't talk to me about a God of love!"

"Buddy Girl, all I'm saying is—"

"My whole life that's all I've ever heard from you and Dad. '*God knows what's best, Ally. God loves you, Ally. God is love, God is love.*' "

"Is that so wrong?"

"It is if it's a lie."

"And if it isn't?" There was a moment's pause. "The Bible is chock-full of—"

"I don't give a rip what the Bible says, Grandpa! Open your eyes. Look around you!"

Dad said nothing.

"You keep saying you're trying to catch God's love in your paintings, and you keep saying you're failing."

He sighed in agreement. "I'm afraid I'm no closer than when I began. He's just too awesome, too—"

"Is He?" She demanded. "Are you so sure? Or is the reason—" She broke into a fit of coughing. "Is the reason . . ." She tried to force out the words, but it was no good and she had to wait until the coughing ceased. "Maybe the reason you can't capture God's love is because it doesn't exist!"

Dad gave no answer. I closed my eyes and silently began to pray. There'd always been such honesty between these two.

That artist connection. And if Dad couldn't reach her, no one could.

At last he continued. Gently. Compassionately. "Ally, I'm not sure why you have this sickness. And I'd be a liar if I claimed—"

"I'm not talking about the cancer," Ally croaked, her voice still raw from the coughing. "I'm talking about life. Look at the world, Grandpa. Look at the killings and the earthquakes and the starving children. You can't turn on the news without seeing some tragedy. And the holocaust—" She stopped to catch her breath, then continued. "The pictures they showed us in school. Six million Jews killed, Grandpa. Six million! And they're supposed to be God's chosen!"

Again, Dad gave no response.

She continued. "I tell you, if that's the way God treats His chosen, then you can take me off His list right now." More coughing. "Take me off the list, 'cause I'm not interested!"

The silence was interminable. When Dad finally spoke his voice was strangely quiet. "We all face seasons of life, Buddy Girl." He hesitated, then resumed. "Some of those seasons are easy and, well, some of them can be pretty hard." Another pause. I could hear him thinking, working it out. "When you stop and consider it, why should our lives be any different from the rest of His creation?"

Ally did not respond. I heard the soft creaking of bedsprings as Dad rose and the groan of the wood floor as he moved toward the window. "It's just like this tree out here," he said. "We all go through seasons. Sometimes we're full of life, sending out new branches, new leaves. Other times, those branches and leaves wither and die. But if we trust Him . . . if we trust Him, He'll always work out those seasons for our best. Always."

For the longest time there was no answer. When Ally finally spoke, her voice was cool and detached. "I'm not interested, Grandpa. I'm not interested in God . . . or His seasons."

"Ally—"

"In fact, Dad, if you're out there, you can come in. Dad? I know you're there. Dad?"

I rose stiffly to my feet. Was I really that predictable? I approached the doorway and stuck in my head as if I'd just been passing by. "You wanted something, sweetheart?"

She gave me a look that said she knew exactly what I'd been up to. Busted again, I sighed and entered.

"You see that tree out there?" she asked, motioning to the window.

I turned to the look. We were now deeply into Fall. Even as she spoke one or two of the yellow and orange leaves fluttered out of sight toward the ground.

"All you and Grandpa ever talk about is how much God is supposed to love us." She turned to her grandfather. "And now you're saying this is just another one of His seasons, that I'm just supposed to have faith and trust Him."

I glanced from Ally to Dad, who was holding her look, waiting for more.

She took an uneven breath and swallowed. "Well, I promise you this. I promise both of you that when the last leaf falls from that tree out there, I'll be gone."

"What?" The outburst came before I could stop it.

She continued, her determination growing. "If God wants me around, if He's got all this love you're always talking about, then all He has to do is keep one leaf on that tree. Just one stupid leaf." She was hit with another spasm of coughing. I took the moment to glance at Dad, but he avoided my eyes. She recovered and continued. "That's not a hard thing for this great God of love to do, is it? Save just one stupid leaf?"

"And ... if He doesn't?" I tentatively asked.

"Then I'll be dead."

"Buddy Girl..." She turned to him. "You can't ... you can't test God like that."

"Why not—He's testing me!"

"But ... He's God."

"Then He'll do whatever He wants with or without my permission." She took another breath and grew all the more resolved. "He can keep a leaf on that tree if He wants ... or He can let them all drop. It's up to Him. But I promise you this: When the last leaf falls, I'll be gone."

The room grew silent. Outside, I could hear the neighbor kids laughing; someone was bouncing a basketball. In the distance was the drone of a leaf blower. Neither Dad nor I spoke. What could we say? My daughter had made up her mind. Her will had been set, and nothing we could say or do would change it. Did it anger God? I don't know. I only hoped that underneath He saw a very frightened little girl trying to make sense out of a very frightening situation. But I did know this: Dad and I were no longer fighting for my daughter's life. Instead, the stakes had just been raised.

Now it appeared we were fighting for her soul.

I opened my eyes. The microwave read 5:28. Two minutes had passed. I rose from the table. It took more effort than I expected. I shuffled to the cupboard and pulled out a mug. I filled it with water and dumped in a spoonful of instant coffee. After putting the cup into the microwave and setting the timer, I did what I had done so many times throughout the night, throughout this entire ordeal: I prayed ... for Ally, for her health, for everything. And, as was my custom, I ended with the phrase: "According to Your will. Amen."

Is such a phrase difficult to pray? Sometimes. But if there was one thing I'd learned over the years, it's that His ways are better than mine. And sometimes, just to remind me, He lets me have my way ... for better or for worse. I leaned against the counter and smiled quietly, recalling one of those "for worse" moments...

It had been about a year before Ally had been diagnosed. She had just received her driving permit. And, once again, exercising my incredible ability to misunderstand my teen, I insisted she learn to drive with a stick shift. Hey, if she could drive a clutch, she could drive anything. It made no difference what Dad or Jen or anybody else had to say, I'd made up my mind. My kid was tough and determined. Every ounce of logic told me she could handle it.

Unfortunately, with teens, "logic" isn't always part of the picture.

"Dad, I'm really not feeling good," she said that fateful Saturday as we headed toward the Toyota pickup sitting in the driveway.

The Toyota pickup that Jeff Brighton had loaned to us for this very occasion.

"Ally, you've been bugging me for months."

"I know, but—"

"But what?"

"Well, I've got a headache, and my stomach is hurting and—"

"Ally..."

"And the only thing they taught us about in Driver's Ed was an automatic."

"No sweat," I said as I opened the door for her to climb in. "This is a breeze."

"Dad..."

Once again I was surprised at how vulnerable this strong-willed child of mine could be, particularly when she was out of her element. But I had made up my mind and nothing could change it.

"Please...," she whined.

I shook my head, walked over to my side, and climbed in. The lesson was about to begin.

Twenty minutes later, when she'd finally found a gear (and worn out Jeff's transmission in the process), we were off. The only problem was, "off" should have involved finding reverse and backing down the driveway ... not dropping into first and leaping forward into the—

"Look out!" I shouted.

No doubt her reflexes would improve with practice, but for now she hit the brakes a split second *after* we hit the garage door.

"Sorry," she cringed.

I nodded, trying not to traumatize her with hysterical shouting. In the meantime I silently began to calculate whether to pay directly for the damages or report it to my insurance company (with a teen driver and increased premiums this could involve taking out a second or third mortgage). A moment passed before Ally finally recovered and, after another wrestling match with the gearshift, found reverse.

"Good," I sighed. "Now gradually let up on the clutch.

She obeyed.

"Gently, gently, there you—"

The pickup leaped backwards. Unfortunately, Ally pan icked, which meant she cranked the wheel too hard to the right, which meant Sammy's bicycle suddenly met the same fate as my garage door.

"Ally!" I cried after she'd hit the brakes.

"Well, it's his fault," she sniffed. "You always tell him not to leave stuff in the front yard!"

I regained my composure and nodded, while adding the cost of a new bicycle to my increased premiums.

At last, we made it out into the street. And gradually, as the morning wore on and Jeff's clutch wore out, Ally began getting the hang of it.

"Gently, gently," I cautioned as we pulled up behind a sleek Lexus on Pinehurst, just a few blocks from the high school.

"Dad, will you quit worrying? I've got it covered. Oh, no—look! There's Tina and Debbie!"

"Who?"

"Over there at the crosswalk!"

I turned.

"Don't look!" she cried.

"But you just told me—"

"Dad!"

I did my best to obey as the light turned green. "Okay now," I said, "release the clutch gradually..."

"I know."

"Easy..."

"Dad, I know!"

"Easy."

"Dad, I—"

"Look out!"

Apparently her version of "I know" wasn't the same as mine. Once again we flew forward, only this time into something far less forgiving than my garage door. As we hit the Lexus, I could feel the sound of crunching metal throughout my body ... particularly in the area of my billfold.

But Ally would not be deterred. After all, those were her friends she was pretending not to see. Somehow rationalizing that she could minimize the damage by quickly backing up, she dropped the pickup into gear, and we shot backwards ... directly into a white soccer-mom van.

"Ally!"

Now she was panicking, though it didn't stop her from yelling, "I know, Dad, I know!" (apparently a reflex response for all teens). Effortlessly, she found first and again we shot forward.

"Ally!"

This time she swerved hard to the left and, thanks to my prayers, missed the Lexus by inches. As we zoomed past I calmly turned to my daughter and, in my most comforting and consoling voice, screamed, "Are you out of your mind? Stop the car!"

"But that's Tina and Deb!" she cried, glancing into the rearview mirror. "Tina and Deb are there!"

"Ally! ALLY!"

We picked up speed.

"Ally, stop the car! Ally!" But by the looks of things we wouldn't be stopping until we ran out of gas. "ALLY!"

Up ahead lay the high school. A couple of kids on bikes were pulling into the intersection.

"LOOK OUT!" I screamed, no longer as worried about traumatizing my daughter as I was about charges of vehicular manslaughter.

This time Ally obeyed. She yanked the wheel and we veered hard to the right, bouncing onto the curb and taking out a postal box in the process. It wasn't until we were up on the high-school lawn and running over the rose garden (which had barely recovered from my rollerblade visit a few years back) that we finally slowed to a stop.

I tried to catch my breath. "Are you all right?" I asked.

"I'm fine, Father," she said in her most condescending tone.

"Are you sure?"

"Of course I'm sure. It's just..."

"It's just what?" I asked, looking her over, feeling rising concern about any injuries she may have incurred.

"You don't think ... I mean Tina and Deb, you don't think they recognized us, do you?"

The timer to the microwave dinged, pulling me from my thoughts and back into the dark kitchen. I took out the mug. The wind continued its dull wail. So many memories. Some sweet, some bitter. Some in this very room...

We had continued to wait one agonizing week after another as Ally's blood count slowly rose high enough for them to operate. Not only were they going to cut away part of her leg and replace it with stainless steel and cadaver bone, but now they would also have to remove the cancer that had advanced to her lungs.

When the time finally arrived, I didn't know whether to be full of joy or to be petrified. As I recall, I was a lot of both ... which would explain why, the night before, it was impossible for me to sleep. I stole down to the kitchen and, in the early morning silence, fixed myself a cup of coffee. I don't know how long I sat at the table, quietly praying, before I was startled at the sound of the screen door groaning open. I looked up, surprised to see Dad entering from the back porch. A freezing gust of November wind surrounded him as he stepped inside.

"Dad?"

He looked up, as surprised as I was. "Paul? It's four o'clock in the morning. What are you doing up?"

"I might ask you the same question," I said.

He grinned and coughed slightly—a cough that had seemed to be growing more frequent the last few days. "I think I've finally found it," he said, rubbing warmth back into his hands.

"It?" I asked.

"The masterpiece." He headed toward the cupboard to grab himself a mug. "After all these years I think I'm finally capturing His love."

I suppose I should have been happy for him, but having a few other things on my mind, the best I could come up with was, "You should take better care of yourself." He said nothing, and I continued. "It's too cold to be wandering between here and the garage in the middle of the night."

"What about you?" he countered. "Didn't the doctor say you needed some rest?"

"Tomorrow's the operation. I'm just sitting here talking with God."

"So was I."

"With your painting?"

He nodded.

I shrugged, in no mood to argue. We all had different ways of communing with God. For me, it was these late-night vigils. For Dad, it was his painting. And if it took a crisis like this to get his creative juices flowing, who was I to object? We each had our own methods of coping.

And what about my wife? How did my rock-steady Italian beauty, who seemed to endure the situation better than any of us, cope? I wish I knew. Oh, I tried to be the good husband and to support her. After all, I was the man of God. But she always seemed to be the one with the strength—taking everything in stride, responding to the day-to-day problems with her simple pragmatic faith. At least in the beginning. But, week after week, month after month, even Jen had started to wear down.

I REMEMBER THE DAY of the operation. Ally had been in surgery nearly five hours. I'd left our family and friends in the waiting room and had gone down to the cafeteria to stretch my legs and get some coffee. When I returned, Jen was nowhere to be found.

"Try the nursery," Jeff suggested. "The Youngrens had their baby last night."

I nodded and headed to the elevator and the maternity ward. *Now, isn't that just like her,* I thought. *Here she is, undergoing impossible pressure, and yet she's found time to minister to a couple in our church who just had their first child. That's so typical,* I thought. *So typical.*

But as I rounded the corner and saw my wife standing with the Youngrens, I realized I'd overestimated her strength. The couple stood at her side, awkward and confused. For, as Jen held their little baby in her arms, she was weeping uncontrollably. Hearing my approach she glanced up and returned the baby to the Youngrens. Tears streamed down her cheeks. She said only two words, but they still break my heart every time I think of them.

"Oh, Paul..." The moan came from deep inside her soul.

Immediately I was beside her, wrapping my arms around her, holding her, feeling her trembling body against mine. There was nothing I could do or say. But I tried. "I know," I whispered. "I know ... I know ... I know..."

Because I did know. We all face our fears differently. We all look to God, pleading and bargaining with Him on different terms and in different ways. At least that was the case with my wife, my father, myself, and everyone else I knew. Well, everyone but Ally.

Because, as far as I knew, my daughter was no longer talking to God at all.

FORTUNATELY, ALLY SAILED THROUGH THE OPERATION WITH flying colors. There were no complications on the operating table and, for the time being, no more medical surprises. There was, however, that devastating final round of chemotherapy. And something even more traumatic. Thanksgiving dinner...

Later, we all found someone to blame. Some thought it was my fault for suggesting Ally invite her friend Ryan over. Others thought it was Jen's mistake for buying the new dishwasher soap that, according to the ads, "Will leave your silverware unbelievably shiny" (not to mention unbelievably slippery). Others blamed Sam for showing off.

I, for one, blamed the sweet potatoes.

Although Ally had pulled through the operation, she hadn't bounced back as quickly as we'd hoped. In fact, both her health and her attitude continued on a downward slide.

Much of this was due to her leg. Although saved and reconstructed, it was misshapen and would never look normal. The doctors did their best—replacing the diseased bone with stainless steel rod and cadaver bone, then covering it with a muscle flap and skin graft. Still, there would always be a huge chunk of flesh missing, making it look, at best, like she'd been the victim of some shark attack. We tried to explain that a deformed leg was better than dying or than having no leg at all. This made perfect sense to any adult—not quite such perfect sense to a teenage girl whose worth is measured mostly by looks and whose sole purpose in life is to dance.

Medically, the doctors attributed her worsening condition to the more powerful chemo they now used to kill any remaining residue of the lung and bone cancer. But I knew her attitude went deeper than any misshapen leg or chemical poisoning. Something inside Ally had given up. That childlike faith of hers that had once been so trusting and accepting was nearly dead. And her health and emotional outlook followed suit.

Now, almost every morning, I caught myself glancing out the window, checking on the thinning leaves of the maple, knowing full well that Ally was doing the same. By Thanksgiving only a few dozen leaves remained. I warned Ally over and over again that you don't test God. And her response?

Over and over again she replied, "When the last leaf falls, I'll be gone."

The meal had started off well enough. Despite the obvious tension regarding her leg (she did her best to keep it covered), everyone seemed to be having a good time. We were all showing off a bit for Ryan, trading jokes and wisecracks. Most were stories to embarrass Ally—you know, the usual childhood stuff. To her credit, she managed to hold her own with zingers about Jen's snoring and my athletic skills (particularly in rollerblading).

Grandpa was in his room getting some rest. His cough had grown worse, and though we were careful never to say it outright, with her weakened immune system from the chemo, there was some concern about him infecting her. And his picture capturing God's love? It had been a long time since I'd seen him so excited. Although he refused to let any of us see it just yet, he was like a little boy, so thrilled, so enthusiastic. Apparently, he was finally painting his masterpiece.

The trouble started when Ally, who sat across the table from Sam, began teasing him about sleeping with Bartholomew, his stuffed koala. Although it was all good natured, I could see the barbs taking their toll on our eleven-year old, wanna-be man. And, lacking his older sister's verbal skills, it was only natural for him to resort to another means of defense...

"Ally," he warned, cocking a forkful of sweet potato in her direction.

But Ally was having too good of a time. "...and we had to turn around and come all the way home 'cause he kept bawling that he couldn't sleep without his woodle, fuzzy-wuzzy Bartholomew."

Sam pulled the fork back further.

"But that's nothing compared to—"

"Ally..."

"—the time he blamed Bartholomew for wetting his bed."

"Ally." Now it was Jennifer's turn to warn her with a discreet frown, "I think that's enough."

"He drank like, what was it, four glasses of lemonade before bedtime and—"

"Ally..."

"—he barely fell asleep before suddenly—"

I'm sure Sam didn't do it on purpose, and as he later insisted, if that dishwashing soap hadn't made the tongs of the fork so slippery, he might have been able to hang on. But one minute Ally was chattering on with impish delight, the next she was shocked into silence, sporting a glob of orange yams on the side of her face.

Now, I know it sounds like we spoil our kids, but we're usually pretty strict. Still, with the tension that had filled our home the past several weeks and the astonished surprise on our daughter's face, well, there wasn't one of us who could stop laughing. It was just too funny. And it was no doubt this lapse of self-control on Jen's and my part that undermined any authority our warnings might have carried. It's hard to be taken seriously when you can't breathe from laughter.

"Ally. . . ," I gasped as I saw her reaching for a biscuit. But, sensing my lack of commitment, she fired off the biscuit, hitting Sam squarely in the forehead before it ricocheted into the gravy bowl and splattered Heather.

"Sam. . ."

Too late. He was already reaching for a green olive to retaliate. If Ally hadn't closed her mouth, it would have landed inside.

"All right," Jen managed to gasp between laughs, "that's enough now!"

Too late, again. Next came a carrot stick . . . or two . . . or three.

"Ally . . . Sam. . ."

Heather was next. Her weapon of choice? Sweet gherkins.

And so it began. Soon Ryan and even Jen and I were involved. It was all-out war, each person fighting for themselves as more yams and biscuits (and I even recall seeing a piece or two of turkey) flew by. At one point I glanced at Jen to make sure she approved, only to discover she was doing the same with me . . . before nailing me with a spoonful of cranberry sauce. We both sensed it, we both *knew* it—like the water fight, this craziness was exactly what our family needed (though I made a mental note to offer Ryan a crisp twenty-dollar bill to make sure word of how Pastor celebrates Thanksgiving remained our little secret).

It had been a long time since I had laughed so hard. Jen, too, for that matter. And the kids, they were in heaven. Green bean casserole, cranberry sauce, anything and everything served as a weapon. Nearly five minutes passed before we'd depleted the ammunition and took a moment to evaluate the damage. The tablecloth was covered with food as our faces and clothes dripped with the festive greens, reds, and browns of various holiday food groups.

Her face wet with tears of laughter, Ally pointed at Ryan. "You look so gross!"

"Me? What about you?" Ryan said, removing a piece of dressing from her hair.

"And what about me?" little Heather asked, her white blouse sporting a healthy portion of mashed potatoes, complete with gravy.

"You look bad too," I assured her.

To which, Sam, never to be outdone, claimed, "I look grosser than all of you put together."

Still laughing, (I think it was the mixture of cranberry sauce and yams in his hair that did it) we all agreed, until Ally suddenly reached for her pants leg. "Oh yeah," she giggled, "you want to see gross?"

Before we could stop her, she had pulled up her pants to reveal her leg.

The laughter faded. To this day I'm not sure why she did it. Nerves, self-consciousness, maybe for one brief moment in time she felt comfortable with who she was, I'm not sure. But, whatever the reason, we all found ourselves staring at the misshapen leg with its bright pink scar tissue and the giant gap of missing muscle.

In Ryan's defense, no one could have been prepared for what he saw so suddenly. And, though he was quick to recover, it wasn't quick enough. Ally had seen the shock of revulsion fill his face. She dropped the pants leg. Tears of laughter suddenly mixing with tears of pain.

"Ally," Jen said.

She pushed herself away from the table and rose.

"Ally. . ."

But Ally wasn't listening. Doing her best to hide her face, she grabbed her crutches, rose and hobbled off. She almost made it to the stairs before the sob escaped. It was only one. But it was enough to break my heart.

"Sweetheart," I pushed back the chair and rose to my feet.

Jen was already on hers. "Ally. . ." Then, giving me one of those "this is a girl thing" looks, she ran to our daughter who had started up the steps.

I stood stunned, unable to speak. Slowly I looked back at the group, at Ryan, at the kids. Everyone stared uncomfortably at the table, none of them sure what to do or how to respond. I knew exactly how they felt. Neither did I.

As the memory faded, I was surprised to see that I had drifted from the kitchen and back into the living room. My gaze wandered to Dad's room, just off the entry hall. The door was shut, as it always was, but that didn't stop my memories...

"Dad, you don't have to leave. You can—"

"Listen," he coughed, "until they find out what's wrong with me, there's no need to stick around and expose Ally."

"I understand that, but—"

He reached down for his bag, and I moved to help. "Here, let me get that."

He shooed me aside. "Get away."

I knew better than to argue. I zipped up my coat and started toward the door. Part of me was angry at him for spending those late-night hours in the studio, for subjecting himself to that freezing air between the two buildings. I'd warned him that he was making himself sick, but he had paid no attention. So what else was new. Then again, if you'd spent your whole life trying to capture the love of God on canvas and it was finally happening, I guess it would be a hard thing to ignore.

"I'll only be in for a day or two, let them run some tests..." He broke into another fit of coughing and slowed to catch his breath. I waited until he stopped before we continued. "Besides, with all the craziness going on around here, I could use the rest."

"I hear that," I said, opening the front door for him.

"Also, rumor has it they've got a couple new nurses," he added.

"Whom I suppose you'll charm into doing your every bidding."

"Usually do." He flashed me that famous uneven grin.

I smiled back, and we stepped into the brittle December air. The temperature hadn't risen above freezing all afternoon.

"And I don't want you messing with my paints while I'm away. No snooping around trying to figure out what I've been working on."

"You mean your masterpiece?" I asked.

He nodded. "It's not quite ready yet. I've got your word—no snooping?"

"No snooping," I agreed.

"Good." He seemed satisfied. "Good."

We stopped one last time in the driveway so he could catch his breath. I took the opportunity to move to the car door and open it for him—something he would never have allowed me to do if he were stronger.

I don't remember much of our conversation after we got into the car. But I do remember the doctor's preliminary diagnosis—pneumonia.

I SHUFFLED TOWARD THE stairway and eased myself down onto the steps. I no longer felt like walking. I took another deep breath, and another—purging breaths, cleansing breaths, the ones I kept hoping would ease the impossible weight on my chest. In my pocket I felt a piece of paper and pulled it out. It was on Ally's stationery. I'd found it on her desk after the paramedics had left. Slowly, I unfolded it. There was a list. Nine items. At the top was the heading:

What I Want to Do Before I Die

It was impossible to tell when she'd written it, though I guessed sometime earlier that evening. I took another breath and quietly read:

Be kissed by Ryan
Hang glide
Eat an extra large, everything-on-it pizza
Warn Heather about boys (the good and the bad)
Like chocolate again
Find out what the big deal about sex is
Own a complete brand-name outfit
Tell Mr. Halstrom he's an idiot for believing in evolution
Tell Mom she's my hero (except when she drives me crazy)

I took another breath, rose from the steps, and turned to start up them. It was time to check on the leaf.

MY FATHER'S DEATH HAD BEEN AS UNEXPECTED AS IT WAS sudden.

I suppose if we hadn't been so focused on Ally and her worsening condition we should have paid more attention to the signs—his coughing, his growing weakness. But, truth be told, I'd never seen him with such peace and contentment, especially when it came to the subject of his painting. Even from his hospital bed...

"I got it," he'd kept saying, "I finally captured His love. Just wait till you see it, you'll be amazed."

We were amazed all right, but not about the painting. We checked Dad into the hospital December 10, and two days before Christmas, December 23, we held his funeral.

For the most part, we all seemed to handle it well. For me the grief came in waves. There were times I actually rejoiced that he was in the presence of his Creator, the very Person he loved more than life itself. Then there were the other times, those moments of utter loneliness and abandonment. All my life, he'd been there for me—to encourage me when I succeeded, to challenge me when I strayed, and to help me back on my feet when I fell.

But now ... now, there was no one. Only God. It was as if the Lord had removed my final crutch, the last of my supports. Now I had to lean solely and completely on Him.

Despite Jen's warning, I spoke at the service. I reminded the packed church that this was a man who loved God with all of his heart and mind. I explained that he was a committed servant who had, just like the Apostle Paul, "fought the good fight ... finished the race ... kept the faith." I continued reading the verse. "Now there is in store for me the crown of righteousness, which the Lord, the righteous Judge, will award to me on that day—and not only to me, but also to all who have longed for his appearing."

I knew these were the words of God and that they were to be trusted. I knew they were truer than life itself. But I also knew that part of me was on autopilot—simply reciting. Hadn't I quoted these same verses at a dozen other services for a dozen other men and women? Did that make them any less true? Of course not. And, yet, as I stood behind the pulpit with my father's body less than ten feet away, I couldn't help thinking how numb and detached I felt. Once again I was playing the part of pastor, watching the entire scene as if I were somewhere else, talking as if I were someone else.

An hour later I spoke at the graveside service—equally as detached, knowing, only by faith, that it was true:

"Do not let your hearts be troubled. Trust in God; trust also in me. In my Father's house are many rooms; if it were not so, I would have told you. I am going there to prepare a place for you. And if I go and prepare a place for you, I will come back and take you to be with me that you also may be where I am."

Throughout the service Ally did her best to avoid my eyes ... as I did hers. Because with every quoted verse, with every handshake, with every spoken assurance of God's love, I could hear her in the back of my mind shouting:

Hypocrite! There is no loving God! When the last leaf falls from that tree I'll be gone!

And the frightening thing was, I had no argument to silence that voice. No logic, no proof, not even feelings. Just faith.

I have fought the good fight . . . I have kept the faith.

That was my battle . . . to keep the faith. Amazingly, here I was, a man of God—a pastor—and yet I was back to the most basic battle of all: *keeping the faith.* How much more of this could I endure? Where was God? Where was His compassion? His grace? Our daughter was slipping away, both physically and spiritually. My closest friend was dead. Now there was nothing. No feeling. No sign of God's love. Nothing.

Only faith. Everything else was stripped. I was being sifted like wheat, poured out like water . . . until all that remained was faith; single-minded, gut-it-out-at-any-cost, faith.

Although I didn't have the courage to look Ally in the eyes, I did keep mental track of where she was. As far as I could tell, she hadn't once approached the coffin to say her final good-byes—neither in the church nor at the graveside. This concerned me since, as I've said, the two had always been so close. Despite her anger and doubts and fears, I felt it was important that she at least reach some sort of closure with the man she so deeply loved.

It wasn't until we were by the limo at the cemetery, saying good-bye to the last of the well-wishers, that I spotted her. She was all alone beside the closed coffin. Everyone else had left. She had waited to be the last one to say good-bye. I would have given anything to know what she was thinking, to hear what she whispered as her lips quietly moved. Was she making her peace with him? With God? I didn't know.

But I would have given anything *not* to see what happened next.

In quiet earnestness, she reached into her shoulder bag and pulled out her newest pair of toe shoes. Silently, she wrapped the silk ankle ribbons about the shoes and set them atop the lid of the casket. Then, without a word, she turned and limped away.

My throat ached. Ally lived to dance. That's all she had ever wanted in life. And now, artist to artist, she had just given up to him the most precious thing in her life. At least that's what I thought at first. But as I watched, a chill crept over me. I shuddered as the real truth took hold. That's not what my daughter was doing. Not at all.

As she hobbled off, I realized Ally wasn't giving up her art. Instead, she was giving up her life.

I trudged up the stairs and headed across the worn carpet. Despite the blowing wind, everything seemed strangely still. Eerily so. I stepped into Ally's room and moved to look out the window. Sheets of water slid down the pane; branches of the tree continued to whip and slap. For the moment, it was impossible to see the leaf. I lifted a hand and placed my palm against the glass, feeling its coldness, feeling the vibration of wind and surging rain. I thought of Peter in the New Testament, of how he tried to walk through a similar storm. And how he succeeded only when he kept his eyes fixed on Jesus, only when he believed in His faithfulness. That's what the leaf had become for us. Yes, there was always the fear that one day we would look and it would be gone. But the fact that it remained day after day, week after week, had also turned it into a symbol of God's faithfulness, a symbol on which we kept our eyes fixed.

At this moment, however, that symbol was no longer visible. And like Peter, when he no longer saw his source of hope in the storm, I felt myself sinking. I dreaded these moments of despair, despised myself for being so weak. Dad would never have been like this. He'd have held true till the end, no matter what the end brought. What had he said? *His love is even greater than death.* And he believed it. With every fiber of his being, he believed it.

Did I?

Not as often as I wished. And certainly not now.

Oh, I still had my moments. Those bright times of faith when I trusted in God regardless of the situation. So did Jen. Though it was interesting during Ally's illness, we seldom had them at the same time. It seemed that whenever I was down, she was up. Whenever she was down, I was up. We'd both noticed this and remembered the verse in Ecclesiastes: "Though one may be overpowered, two can defend themselves. A cord of three strands is not quickly broken." And between myself, Jen, and our Lord, we were never broken. Frayed, yes. Worn to the point of snapping, no doubt. But never entirely broken. Not even in February, though that was the closest—the time Jen had nearly lost it...

As I said, the increased potency of the final chemotherapy had left Ally weaker and more susceptible to infection than ever before. This by itself was traumatic enough. But then, at the end of January, the doctors told us she had to go back in again for a minor operation to do some "cleaning up." They assured us it was not as major as the first time, but for us the stress was even greater. Would it ever end, this continual assault?

After Dad's death we somehow went through the motions of Christmas. The holidays were always Jen's specialty, and she would not be deterred by something as trivial as death or disease. But after the holidays came and went, after the decorations were put away, and we prepared for another operation, the doubts of my beloved wife finally reached critical mass...

"DAD..." SAM'S VOICE SOUNDED frightened over the telephone. "You've got to come home! Mom, she's..."

"What?" I asked. "What about Mom?"

"She's gone crazy! She's locked herself in Grandpa's studio and there's all sorts of banging and noise and stuff!"

"Are you sure it's Mom?"

"Yeah, she's screaming and shouting and everything."

"Hang on, Son. I'll be right there."

I reached home in record time, grateful that there were no police between the church and the house (and just as grateful there were no congregation members). I bounced into the driveway, leaped out of the car, and raced to the side garage door. Sam and Heather were there waiting in tears.

"Are you guys okay?"

They nodded.

I tried the door. It was locked. "Jen?" I called.

There was a loud crash inside. The kids looked at me nervously.

I banged on the door. "Jen, are you in there?"

"What do You want from us?" I heard her yelling from inside. "Just tell me what You want!"

"Jen?"

"She's been shouting like that for half an hour," Sammy said.

"And throwing stuff," Heather added.

Sammy nodded. "Lots of throwing."

I pounded on the door again. "Jen!"

"Just tell me what You want! Just tell me—"

"Jen?"

There was a moment of silence.

"Jen?"

"Paul, is that you?" Suddenly she sounded calm, almost composed. "What are you doing home? Is it 5:00 already?"

"Are you all right?"

"Me? Oh, yeah." There was a strange airiness to her voice. "I'm just having a little talk with God, that's all."

"Can you open the door?"

"Mom?" Sammy called.

"Oh hi, sweetheart. Is your homework done?"

"Jen, open the door."

"Uh," she cleared her throat, "I don't think now would be a good time for that."

It was Heather's turn, "Mommy..."

"Mommy's okay, honey. Are you wearing your coat?"

I glanced at Heather, not noticing until then that she was shivering in a T-shirt.

"You know better than to come outside without your coat," Jen admonished.

I looked on, amazed. How did she know?

"Mom," Sammy called again.

"Mommy will be out in just a few minutes," she said, then called to me. "Paul?"

I took my cue. I put an arm around each of their shoulders and started directing them toward the house. "It's okay," I said. "Mom's just talking to God. She's just praying; she'll be done soon."

"Praying?" Sammy asked skeptically. "I sure never heard anybody pray like that before."

"Yes, well, uh, Mom's Italian, right?"

"So?"

"So sometimes that's the way they pray in Italy."

"Really?"

I said nothing, hoping the "story" would last until I got them into the house. I'd worry about clearing up ethnic stereotypes later.

"Isn't the Pope in Italy?" Heather asked as we walked up the porch steps.

"Yes, that's right."

"I never saw him pray like that."

"That's 'cause he's too old," Sammy explained.

"Huh?"

"They pick 'em old so when they really get worked up praying and stuff they won't break things. Isn't that right, Dad?"

I raised an eyebrow, impressed at my son's logic. "Well," I cleared my throat, "the Vatican does have a lot of expensive artwork..."

"See?" Sammy said.

Heather nodded, satisfied with the explanation. I opened the door, and they stepped into the kitchen. After assuring them I'd be right back, I turned and headed toward the garage. When I arrived I tapped gently on the door. "Jen?"

There was no answer.

"Jen?" I tried the knob but it was still locked. "Jen, I need you to open up. Jen?"

Panic started to rise, but I swallowed it back. I reached into my pocket, pulled out my keys, and quickly flipped through them. Church door, church office, staff room... "Jen?" Car ignition, car trunk, front door... Why is it the older we get, the more keys we acquire? Padlock to fence, back door... ah, there it was. "Jen?" Still no answer. I inserted the key and pushed open the door.

"Jen?"

The studio was a war zone. Anything that could be tipped over had been tipped over. Easels, stools, a stepladder. Framed canvases, some finished, some not, all strewn across the floor. Stacks of completed paintings that had once leaned neatly against walls and inside the cupboards were scattered everywhere.

"Jen?"

At last I spotted her. She was on the floor, off in the corner, her knees pulled to her chest. She rested her forehead on them. Her thick black hair was disheveled, and a smear of white paint ran across one forearm.

"You okay?" I asked, quietly approaching.

She gave a vague nod.

"You two must have had quite a talk."

She sniffed. "It wasn't bad."

I knelt by her side. I knew better than to touch her, at least for the moment. "Anything you want to tell me?"

There was a brief pause before she raised her head. Her eyes were red and puffy. A trace of blue paint ran across her forehead and down her right cheek. She shrugged. "Not really."

I nodded, waiting in silence until she was ready.

Finally she spoke. "Ryan broke up with Ally today."

"Broke up?" I asked. "I didn't even know they were going steady."

"He still wants to be friends."

I winced. "They still use that old line?"

"And he wondered..." She swallowed. "He wondered if it was okay with her if he asked Isabel to the Winter Prom."

"Her best friend?"

Jen said nothing. I took a deep, incredulous breath. "Well, he's certainly courteous, I'll give him that."

No response. Finally, I reached out my hand. She looked at it a while, then took it. Silently, I helped her to her feet. We stood there in the stillness, surveying the damage. This, I realized, was the first time I'd entered the studio since Dad's death.

When Jen spoke, her voice was a raspy whisper. "When will it end, Paul?"

I said nothing.

"When will He quit torturing us?"

I frowned but did not respond.

Several seconds passed before she continued, "It's not here, you know."

"What's that?"

"His painting."

"The 'masterpiece'?"

She nodded. "There's nothing here. At least not like he talked about."

I turned to her. "How can you be sure?"

She motioned to the mayhem before us. "I checked."

"But he was so excited," I said. "You heard the way he went on. 'I've finally captured God's love.' In the end that's all he talked about."

"That's all he talked about, but there's nothing here." She took two, three steps away from me. "Just the same old landscapes." She motioned toward the canvases surrounding us. "Just like the ones he always painted. There's nothing special about these, Paul. Not special in the way that he talked about."

"But he was so certain he'd captured it—God's love."

Another moment passed before she answered. "Maybe he was only fooling himself." Her voice grew thinner. She looked everywhere, anywhere, but at me. "Maybe we're all fooling ourselves. Maybe that love, maybe it really doesn't exist . . . except in our minds." She took an unsteady breath. "Like Dad, maybe we're so busy trying to convince ourselves that it exists, that we fool ourselves into believing it does."

"No. . ." I shook my head. "No, that's not true."

"Isn't it?" Her words sounded more detached. Finally, she let her eyes meet mine. They were as empty as her voice. "Show it to me, then. Show me the proof of God's love."

"What do you—"

"This great, unbelievable love that He's supposed to have for us. Show me."

"Show you?"

"Yes, show me. Where is it."

I scowled. "Well, I suppose the first place to look at—"

"Show me, Paul."

"—is the cross. Jesus' sacrifice on the cross. There's no greater love than what He did for us on the cross."

"And where is that love now?" Her voice grew more focused. "Show it to me. Today, Paul. Show it to me where I live and breathe today."

"Show it to you? How can I show you something like that?"

She snorted.

I took a half step toward her. "It's not something I can show you. It's something you have to believe. You know that. It's something we've got to accept on faith."

She slowly turned from me and looked back across the paintings. "Then I'm afraid I've about run out of faith, my friend."

I stood, unable to speak. Several moments passed before she composed herself enough to turn and start to exit.

"Jen? Jennifer?"

She did not answer until she arrived at the door. Then turning back, she responded with that same detached voice. "Maybe Ally's right, Paul. Maybe that love really doesn't exist. And maybe, like your father here, maybe we're all just fooling ourselves into believing that it does."

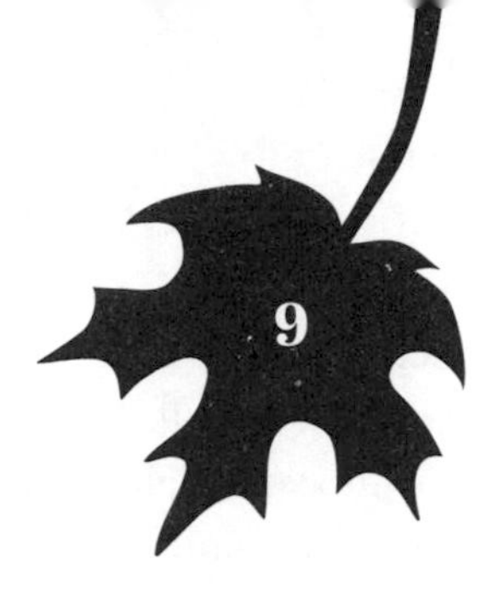

STILL STANDING AT ALLY'S WINDOW, LOOKING OUT INTO THE storm, I was again struck by the loneliness. The absolute abandonment. No longer was I able to rely on Dad's wisdom and experience. No longer was I able to rely on Jen's faith. In fact, for now, even the leaf was impossible to see. Tears welled up in my eyes as the all-too-familiar constriction filled my throat. I scolded myself for the self-pity and tried to shake it, but the feeling of isolation kept growing.

I turned from the window and looked back across Ally's room. It was just as the paramedics had left it—blankets thrown onto the floor, mattress cockeyed, plastic wrappers lying about from the needles they'd shoved into her veins.

The ordeal had been less than an hour ago. I could still hear Jen's voice behind me, shouting at the crying children to stay away, to go back into their rooms. I had stood at this very spot, helplessly watching strangers work over my daughter's unmoving body, hearing their calm, matter-of-fact tones, not missing the underlying tension as they fought to bring her back. It had been a nightmare that I watched, paralyzed and dumb, as they pulled her to the floor (the very floor on which we used to kneel and say her prayers), as they ripped off her pajama top, revealing her pale nakedness, as they applied jelled paddles to the chest with its protruding ribs, as they called out some number, as her body convulsed, jerking crazily like a lifeless doll. And, when there was no response, starting the same procedure all over again—here in my house, in my daughter's room, her inner sanctum.

Then she was on a gurney rattling past me, her face wet and white. Thin clumps of hair plastered to a damp skull, eyes shut. Coldness enveloping me. Sammy and Heather still crying hysterically, Jen still screaming at them to go back to their rooms, their clinging fiercely to me, her fighting to pry them off. The terror, the chaos, the panic. . .

I stood alone in the room, closing my eyes, trying to push the scene from my memory. Had it really come to that? Our faith, our "Christian maturity," degenerating into nothing more than uncontrollable fear, hysterical screaming? When the facade was gone, when all of the Christian varnish was finally stripped away, was that all there was, was that all we were made of?

I felt myself starting to sway. I opened my eyes to regain my balance. And there it was . . . on her nightstand. The ten-inch porcelain ballerina. A gift from Dad. It was one of the few dance mementos she'd kept. But in the hustle and bustle, the paramedics had apparently knocked it over. And now, like some malicious taunt, it lay broken and shattered on the table.

The doll began floating, wavering in my tears as I moved toward it. I knelt, reaching for it, surprised at how violently my hands shook. Despair overtook me, sucking me under, trying to drown me. Another wave of dizziness hit. I had to reach for the bed to steady myself. A sob escaped from my throat. I was surprised at the sound, but before I could recover, another came, more violent—so strong, so deep that it pulled breath from my lungs. Others followed. I tried to swallow them back, but they wouldn't stop. I shoved a fist into my mouth, muffling the sound so I wouldn't wake Sammy and Heather. And still they came.

Stop it! This is not how a pastor behaves! Stop it! This is not acceptable behavior!

I tried to rise, but my legs betrayed me, buckling until I was back on the floor. Embarrassed, loathing my weakness, I tried again. The results were the same. All I could do was stay on my knees and lean on her mattress.

How pathetic. A man of faith? Who was I kidding? There was no faith here. Not any more. Maybe there never had been. Maybe, like Jen had said, I'd only been fooling myself.

Another sob came, so violent that I gagged.

Again I tried to rise and failed. I leaned over the bed, pressing my wet face into her sheets. And there I wept. What a charade I lived. Suddenly, it was so obvious, so plain. I was a fraud. A charlatan. I'd fooled myself, my congregation, and more despicably I'd fooled my wife and children.

"I can't do this," I gasped. "I've made a mistake. Please..." Another sob escaped. "I don't have the faith for this. I don't have ... please..."

Then give Me what you have.

The words shocked me. I knew they came from my mind, but I also knew they were not my thoughts.

"I have nothing ...," I groaned. "I have no faith ... just a dying daughter ..."

Then give Me what you have.

The request angered me. I whispered fiercely, "I have nothing! A worthless faith, a dying daughter!"

"We have nothing, oh Lord, just two fish and some loaves of bread."

I recognized the phrase immediately. From the Gospels. It was the disciples' response when Jesus had commanded them to feed the five thousand.

"We have nothing."

Jesus had asked them to do the impossible, and they had no resources to accomplish it. Just two fish and some loaves of bread.

Then give to Me what you have.

A dull understanding began to stir. Was it possible? Like the disciples, I had nothing to give Him—just worthless leftovers, a shattered faith, a dying daughter.

Then give Me what you have.

All those years of ministry, my life as a pastor, as a man of God—suddenly they no longer counted, suddenly they were nothing but leftovers, broken, worthless. A life I once thought so good and righteous had revealed itself as completely empty, as totally—

Then give Me what you have.

"I have nothing!" I cried. "I am nothing! Can't you see that! I have nothing to give!"

Then give Me what you have.

My body shook. Why did He keep tormenting me? Didn't He understand that I had nothing to give?

Then give Me what you have.

"But I have—"

Then give Me what you have.

"All right!" I shouted. "All right, take it!" I was breathing faster, harder. My heart pounded in my ears. The words tumbled out more quickly, as if I'd entered some unknown current, something swift and powerful, pulling the thoughts from my brain faster than I could think them. "Do with her whatever You want! I can't believe anymore! I can't hang on anymore! If You want my baby, take her. She's Yours. If You want my job, my faith, my life, take it! Take everything! Your will, not mine!" I began crying again, but this time I was unable to stop. The anger had dissolved into helpless resignation. "Your will, Lord.... Your will, Your will, Your will..."

I don't know how long I lay there weeping, my face on the wet sheet. I don't know how long I prayed that prayer. But gradually, as I continued to give her up, as I continued giving Him everything, relief began to flow into me. Not the relief of victory, but the relief of giving up, of turning it over.

And dear Lord, we dedicate to You this day, little Allison Marie Newcombe... They were the words I'd prayed nearly eighteen years earlier at Ally's dedication. *...for You to use for Your glory, oh Lord. For You to accomplish Your greatest purpose.*

And those words were still true. She was still His. She'd always been His. Somehow over the years I'd just forgotten and taken her back. But the words spoken then had the same truth as the ones I'd just cried from my knees. Ally was not mine. Nor were my struggles to believe mine. They were His. All of it His. *His* daughter. *His* struggles. *His* faith. "Your will be done." I'd said those words a thousand times, but only now they were becoming real. If He wanted to take her home, so be it. If He wanted my broken sham of a life, my threadbare faith, so be it. We were His. Whatever He chose I would accept. Completely. Without reservation.

"Not my will, oh Father, but Yours."

And with the relief of giving up, came freedom. Lightness. As if some huge weight were being removed from my chest.

"Not my will..." Whatever He chose, with Ally, with myself, with everything, "...but Yours."

The resolution grew stronger, taking hold. We were back to square one. Only this time it was real, greater than any words, deeper than any theology. Because this time it was from the heart. "Not my will, but Yours." I took a ragged, uneven breath. "Not my will, but—"

"Paul?"

The voice surprised me. At first I wasn't even sure I'd heard it.

"Paul? You up here?"

I raised my head. Somebody was coming up the stairs.

"Paul?"

It was Jeff Brighton. "In—," my voice caught, and I cleared it. "I'm here in Ally's room."

"We knocked but nobody answered, so we—" He appeared in the doorway, all 250 pounds of him. "You look awful."

I tried to smile. "Thanks." With effort, I was able to push myself from the bed and rise to my feet. "Actually, I think I'm doing a little better," I said, wiping my face with my hands.

He looked at me skeptically.

But it was true. I was feeling lighter, freer, more than I had in a very long time.

"Jeff?" It was Sally.

"Up here, hon," he called.

She appeared beside her husband, her plump, usually cheery face creased with a deep frown. "You okay, Pastor? How are the kids?"

"Asleep, I hope."

"And Ally?"

I shook my head. "No word. But I can tell you this much." They looked at me. "I can tell you she's definitely in God's hands."

They both gave the expected nods, but I knew they hadn't heard, not really. I knew for them it was still words . . . still theory and religion. They hadn't yet experienced the reality, that absolute assurance, that was solidifying in my heart. How could they? How can anyone take God's truths and make them part of their heart? How does anyone take the Word of God and make it flesh? Maybe we don't. Maybe we can't. Maybe that job belongs to the Creator of the heart.

"Can you drive?" Jeff was asking.

I turned to him, not entirely hearing.

He repeated himself. "I can take you if you want. Sally will stay here with the kids, and I can—"

"No," I shook my head. "I can drive."

They stood a moment, unconvinced.

I wiped my face. "I'm okay, really." I tried to smile, then forced myself into action. "But I better get going."

They nodded. We exchanged brief hugs and I headed out of the room. But I'd barely started down the hall before Jeff called out, "It's still there, I see."

"What?" I turned to find both of them looking out the window.

"The leaf."

"It is?"

He pointed. "Didn't you see it?"

I came back to join them. But, even as I approached, I noticed some of the old apprehension was missing. The anxiety of searching for the leaf, the fear of not being able to find it was no longer as strong. God would do what God would do. And it would be for the best. The leaf would be there or it would not be there. Whatever He chose, whether it was to heal her or take her, it would be for the best . . . because it would come from His great love.

Then His love will be even greater than her death. Dad's words rang in my head. The ones he'd spoken to me in his studio at the beginning of this ordeal. And now, for the first time, their truth was starting to make sense.

"See," Jeff pointed, "right there."

The rain had lessened. The faintest hint of dawn glowed gray in the jet-black sky. And there, where it had always been, just above the garage roof, I caught glimpses of the last leaf, standing bravely by itself. Don't get me wrong—the relief was still there, but my desperation wasn't nearly as great. By giving up, it was as if I'd been freed. The burden was no longer mine. If God wanted that leaf to stay, then that would be for the best. If God wanted that leaf to fall, then somehow, as painful as it would be, I knew that would also be for the best.

His love will be greater than her death.

I headed down the stairs, still a little shaky, hanging onto the railing for support.

"Call us when there's news," Sally said.

I nodded, grabbed my coat from the hall closet, and headed out into the storm. The blast of cold and wet was a shock. Yet it felt fresh, almost invigorating, as if . . . as if I were being baptized . . . all over again.

Your will be done.

I climbed into the car and started for the hospital, again marveling at the power of those four simple words—how true, how liberating. God was in charge to do whatever He wanted. And in exchange for giving Him that authority, I received His freedom.

Your will be done.

I'd heard those words since I was a child. Not only had Jesus spoken them in the Garden of Gethsemane when He pled for His life, but He also spoke them in the Lord's Prayer: "Your Kingdom come, *Your will be done...*"

But now . . . now they resonated with truth. Now they had finally taken root in my heart. His words had become a reality in my flesh. *My* flesh. *His* words, *my* flesh. The two, at least for the moment, had become one.

How long would this feeling remain? I didn't know. Would I be able to hang onto the freedom? I wasn't sure. But it stayed with me as I sped down the highway. It remained as I squealed into the emergency parking lot with a bit more aggression than befits a pastor. (And why not? If I'd turned everything over to God, that would include my precious reputation, wouldn't it?) And it remained with me as I crossed the storm-littered lot and entered through the hissing hospital doors.

"Pastor..."

I looked up to see Mr. and Mrs. Frampton. They looked tired, frayed, as if they'd been there all night. How deeply I admired them. I didn't always appreciate their theology, but when it came to their love, they had no equal.

"How is she?" I asked.

"Healed in Jesus' name," they said in near perfect unison.

I said nothing. They stayed by my side as we headed towards the lobby.

Mrs. Frampton continued. "We've been praying and believing all night that she is healed, and I know—"

"I don't want you to pray that," I said.

"What?"

"Not any more."

"But, Pastor—"

Still feeling the boldness from my revelation, I continued. "I want you to pray that His will and only His will be done. I want you to turn her over to God."

"But . . . don't you want your daughter healed?"

The question slowed me to a stop. I looked at their perplexed stares, then shook my head. "No." They both stifled a gasp. "I want what God wants. And if He wants her healed, I can't think of anything better. But, if for some greater reason, He wants to take her home, then I would rather have that."

"But—"

"I want His most perfect will done here, guys. Do you understand? Nothing less. Pray for His perfect will."

I could already hear the tongues wagging back at church—*The man didn't even want us to pray to save his own daughter*—but the gossip didn't matter. Like everything else, it was now His.

"Paul."

I looked to see Jen coming down the hall, her sister on one arm, a family friend on the other. I quickly joined them. "Are you okay?"

She nodded, though I knew it was a lie, part of that all-too-familiar facade.

"How's Ally?"

She swallowed and for the briefest moment my heart sank. Finally, she spoke. "She's awake a little, if you want to see her."

"Great."

"She's down the hall, room 120."

I glanced anxiously toward the corridor and, reading my mind as she always did, Jen answered, "You go ahead. I'll catch up."

I nodded and practically sprinted down the blue and gray carpet. I spotted the room number and rounded the corner. And then a wave of weakness hit me. The freedom, the elation, started to fade. There was my child, my firstborn, lying tiny and alone in the sterile white bed. Her only companions were the IV stands, the monitors, and the various hardware attached to and hovering around her body.

I pulled myself together and stepped toward the bed. Her eyes fluttered, then opened.

"Hey, Sport," I said, searching for a safe place to hold her hand amidst the IVs. I knelt to her level.

She closed her eyes, then opened them.

"You got quite a set up here," I said. "More wires than the back of our VCR."

Again she blinked. After a moment, I saw her lips try to move.

"What?" I brought my head closer. "What are you saying?"

Again she blinked and again she moved her lips.

I placed my ear beside her mouth, listening intently. I didn't hear a voice, just the faintest puff of breath. "Is. . ." She swallowed and tried again. "Is it. . ."

I smiled. "Yes, it is, sweetheart. It's still there. I saw it just before I left. I don't know how, with the wind and rain and storm, but the leaf is still there."

The corners of her mouth turned in the slightest trace of a smile. Once again, she closed her eyes. But this time she did not reopen them.

I reached up and stroked her patchy clumps of downy hair. Tears spilled onto my cheeks. And gradually the feeling returned. "Your will," I whispered hoarsely. "Your will, Your will, Your will. . . ."

There was worship in those words. And victory. Because we had won. By turning it over to Him, His love would reign . . . regardless. Even if it came to the unbearable heartache of my child dying. *Then His love will be greater than her death.*

"Paul?"

I turned to see Jen standing at the door. I rose and moved toward her, wiping my face with my sleeve. We fell into an embrace. "It's okay," I whispered, "it's going to be all right. Everything is going to be all right." And, as I held her, I noticed that the sky outside was a lighter gray. Morning had arrived. And by the looks of things the storm had finally passed.

10

PASTOR NEWCOMBE?"

I started awake, then glanced around, trying to get my bearings. I was in the hospital. Ally's room. I'd dozed off in one of the chairs beside her bed.

"Yes?" I said, sitting up, doing my best to pretend I hadn't been asleep.

It was Dr. Lawson. Jen was already reaching for my hand.

"The fever's broken," the doctor said. "It was close, but the crisis is over. She's down to 101, and it's still dropping. Looks like we're out of the woods."

I remember leaping up, but I can't remember if I hugged Dr. Lawson first or my wife. All I know is that when I held Jen, her face was as wet as mine. "Thank You, Jesus," I heard her whisper. "Thank You..."

I nodded, adding my own prayer of thanks.

Ally's response came two and a half hours later when she finally woke up. Jen was the first to see her eyes open.

"Paul, look."

Immediately I was hovering over her, stroking her head, making a big deal about what a fighter she was and how good she looked. She endured my gushing as best she could. Then, when she could stand no more, she responded in what could only be described as vintage Ally:

"Tell Sam to keep his hands off my CDs."

BECAUSE OF THE SERIOUSNESS of the infection, nearly a week passed before she was allowed to return home. To Ally's credit, she never grumbled or complained. As determined as she'd once been to give up and die, she now seemed equally as determined to get well and get out of there. It was as if the fever and the storm had become the turning point—not only for her illness, but for her attitude. And why not? The impossible had happened. Against all odds, against a long, harsh winter, against an incredibly fierce storm, the leaf had remained. God had stooped down to this seventeen-year-old girl and, whether it met our prescribed theology or not, He had reached out to her with a love she could understand.

Now, for her, it was simply a matter of getting well and getting on with life.

And getting on she did. Not only with her health, but with deeper matters as well...

On her third day at the hospital she turned to me and said, "When you get a chance, will you bring me my Bible?"

I stared a moment, not believing my ears. Even in areas of the spirit she was determined to recover and make up for lost time. "No rush," she said, feigning her usual casualness, "just the next time you stop by or something."

"Next time I stop by" nothing. After calmly leaving her room I ran down the hall, raced home, dug out her Bible, and returned in record time. I had to make up some excuse about coming back so quickly, but, of course, she immediately saw through it. But instead of calling me on it as she used to, or at least giving me her famous eye roll, she simply smiled a knowing smile (the very one Jen uses when she catches me) and quietly thanked me. It was a little thing, that tiny gesture of knowing kindness, but I'll never forget it. To me it was a clear sign that, though I may not have lost my little girl to disease, I had lost her to something even more formidable: I'd lost her to maturity. Somehow, over the past several months, my self-centered, *I-expect-the-world-to-revolve-around-me* teenager, had become a thoughtful, responsible adult.

Well, usually...

On Tuesday morning we had her all packed and ready to go home. However, the hospital hit several snags and the three of us didn't get out of there until after lunch. Irritated at the inefficiency, Ally wasn't in a great mood. The mood got no better when we finally pulled into our driveway, and she saw Ryan sitting on the front steps.

"Well, look who's here," I said, trying to sound casual as I brought the car to a stop.

"Oh, brother," was all I heard.

Followed by Jen's admonition, "Be nice."

"Hey, Ryan," I called, opening my door as he loped over to greet us.

"Hello, Pastor. Hello, Mrs. Newcombe."

Jen gave a polite smile. "Ryan."

I stepped out and headed back to open Ally's door.

"Hey, Ally," he called, taking a nervous step closer.

"What are you doing here?" she asked as I reached down and helped her to her feet.

"I, uh, I brought you these." He thrust out a slightly wilted bouquet, something he'd obviously bought at the grocery store hours earlier.

"Aren't you supposed to be in school?" she asked.

He moved to her other side to give me a hand, and we headed toward the house. "I took an unexcused absence."

"It's test week."

"Well, yeah."

"That was pretty stupid."

He shrugged. It was obvious she wasn't making this easy for him. And, though it counted for nothing, she definitely had my approval.

"I've been here all morning," he volunteered, hoping to play the martyr.

It didn't work. "You should have called," was all she said.

He gave another shrug.

Silence stole over the conversation. And, taking Ally's cue, it was a silence I made no attempt to break. Jen had already entered the house. We followed, not far behind.

He tried again. "I, uh ... I was looking for that leaf of yours." He glanced overhead toward the maple as we walked between the garage and the house. "Where exactly did you say it was?"

"You can't see it from here," she said. "It's my special leaf, you can only see it from my window." We started up the porch steps.

"Oh, yeah. I think you said that."

More silence. She was good. Very good.

Finally, we arrived at the back door. I opened the screen, starting to help her inside, and she freed her arm from Ryan. "We've got it from here," she said, leaning her weight upon me and hobbling through the door.

"Oh," he cleared his throat. "Okay..."

More awkward silence.

"Thanks for the flowers."

"Oh . . . sure."

"We'll see you."

"Oh . . . okay."

With that she turned, reached out, and gently shut the door in his face.

"Nice work," I said as we made our way through the kitchen toward the stairs.

"He'll be back," she said.

"He will?"

"Don't you know anything about guys?"

"Well, it's been a while..."

"Trust me, he'll be back." Then, flashing me a mischievous twinkle, she added, "If he's worth having, he'll be back."

She was right. He did come back. Soon Ryan was at the house every afternoon, bringing her homework, tutoring her through subjects she'd missed. And Ally's response? She was just grateful enough (not to mention elusive enough) to keep the poor guy continually off balance. In short, he didn't stand a chance. What's the old saying, "He kept chasing her until she caught him"? By the looks of things, that's exactly what was happening. Yes, sir, my daughter had become a woman in more ways than I had ever imagined—or would ever understand.

Spring approached, and Ally grew stronger, with virtually no more setbacks. Though this was no surprise to those of us who knew her. She'd simply set that iron will of hers toward getting well so, of course, she got well. Dr. Lawson and others cautioned us not to let our hopes run away with us, but they obviously didn't know who they were dealing with.

In some ways, neither did we...

It was Easter morning, just about dawn, when I heard Ally's muffled shouting. "Mom ... Dad, come out here!"

My eyes exploded open.

"Guys, you gotta see this!"

I threw off the covers and staggered from our bed in a panic—not entirely asleep, but not entirely awake, either.

"Mom! Dad!"

It took a moment, but in my confusion I finally realized she wasn't shouting from her room, she wasn't even shouting from inside the house. She was shouting to us from outside! I eventually made it to the window and spotted her down in the backyard. She wore a winter coat that she'd thrown over the sweats which had become her permanent sleep uniform. I reached for the window latch, fumbling to undo it.

"Paul...," Jen's bleary voice called from the bed. "What's going on?"

"I don't know." The latch finally gave way, and I pushed up the window. The air was sharp and cold, clearing any remaining sleep from my head. "Ally," I whispered down to her, "what are you doing?"

"You gotta see this," she shouted.

I winced at her loudness and instinctively glanced toward the neighbors. "It's. . ." I held up my watch, trying to focus my eyes, ". . .5:50 in the morning."

"Come on down," she motioned, "you've got to see this."

"Paul," Jen called, "what's going on?"

I turned toward her. "It's Ally. She wants us to see something outside."

Suddenly, I was struck with concern. She still hadn't entirely recovered from her illness, and the last thing she needed was to expose herself to this cold morning air. I turned back to the yard. "Ally—"

"Come on! You've got to see this."

I knew any more arguing would be worthless so, with a fair share of grumbling, I slipped into a pair of shoes, grabbed my robe, and started for the door. I'd barely made it into the hall before I heard Jen crawling out of bed and following. I waited a moment, and together we clomped down the stairs, through the family room, and into the kitchen. I opened the back door, pushed the screen, which groaned at such an early awakening, and stepped out onto the porch. The first glint of sunrise stabbed my eyes. Though the air was sharp and crisp, it was still possible to smell the early signs of spring.

"Over here!" Ally was heading behind the garage, a no-man's-land of blackberry brambles and weeds that I'd always found some excuse not to clean out. And for good reason—the only ones who ever saw that part of the garage were the squirrels and raccoons from the overgrown woods behind and beside us.

"Ally," I protested. She didn't answer. We stepped down the porch steps, following. "What's going on?"

"Over here," she repeated, then disappeared behind the garage.

Reluctantly, Jen and I traipsed through the wet grass, making our way toward the heavily shaded back. We negotiated the corner just in time to see her disappear around the far side, the side no one ever saw, much less visited.

"Ally? Ally!"

No response. With a sigh that I hoped was loud enough for her to hear, we followed, staying close to the building, trying to avoid the weeds and brambles. As we rounded the corner we were blinded by sunlight . . . and Ally. She stood, silhouetted in the morning glare, pointing up to the roof. "Look."

I shielded my eyes and saw our old wooden ladder leaning against the back of the blistered building. It jutted above the gutter two or three feet. On the gutter rested a long, flat board that stretched out from both sides of the ladder. In the morning sun and shadow, the vertical ladder and horizontal plank formed a rough type of cross, nearly perfect in its proportion. But it's what rested on top of the plank that caught our attention.

"What on earth?" Jen asked.

I swallowed. "Ally, are those . . . are those Grandpa's paints?"

She nodded. "Sure looks like it." She pointed to a tipped container with brushes spewing from it. "Those are his brushes.

And over there on the other side of the ladder, aren't those some of his old paint tubes?"

I stepped closer, looking up. She was right. But why? What had he been up to? And on this side of the garage that nobody dared visit. I threw a look at Jen who was frowning. Then at Ally, who had moved to the ladder. She was still too weak to climb, but I wasn't. "Come on," she ordered. "Go on up, and see what he was doing."

I approached and grabbed hold of the ladder. Its wooden rungs felt wet and cold.

"Go ahead," she urged.

I nodded and began. As I climbed, white puffs of my breath glowed in the sun. I reached the top and the board lying over the gutter. But there was nothing more to see—just the spilled can of brushes and the half-empty tubes of paint.

"What's up?" Ally called.

I shook my head. "Nothing." I looked to both sides, then toward the top of the pitched roof. "Nothing, at all."

"How about the other side?"

"Why would he set the ladder up here if he was going over to the other side?"

"Maybe he didn't want us to know."

"Ally..." I protested.

"Please, Dad? You're up there already, just go on over and check it out."

I sighed in exasperation though, truth be told, I was just as curious as she. I climbed up from the ladder and onto the roof.

"Be careful, Paul."

I nodded, working my way up the steep slope of gritty asphalt tiles. I continued looking for signs, for any clue as to what he'd been up to. But I saw nothing, just the usual wear and tear of a roof that obviously needed repair. As I approached the peak of the roof, our house came into view from the other side. Straight ahead of me, two dozen feet away, I could see Ally's window. The light from her room was still on.

"See anything?" Ally asked.

"Not yet."

At the top, I looked down over the other side. And there it was, just to my left and three feet down from the ridge of the roof...

The familiar yellow, orange, and brown of Ally's leaf.

For a moment I did not move. I could only stand there, silently breathing the white plumes of breath.

"Paul? Are you all right?"

I continued to stare.

"Dad?"

I crawled over the ridge of the roof and down the other side until my face was within inches of the painting. Incredible. There on the asphalt tiles was the perfect replica of an autumn leaf—the veins, the colors, the browning around the tips, and his use of light and shadow to give it a three-dimensional look ... all of it was amazing. Even at close range, the painting looked astonishingly real.

I looked from the painting to Ally's window and back again—and noticed even more evidence of Dad's genius. Not only had he painted an exact replica of a leaf, but he'd perfectly positioned it, placing it so the pitch of the roof blocked it from the ground. But that was only the beginning. He'd also set it strategically behind a large limb so that other leaves from that limb would initially block its view as he painted it, while at the same time using that same limb to prevent the leaf from being viewed from any other window in the house. Any window but Ally's. From her window it appeared to be attached to the very limb that blocked it from the other vantage points. It was an exquisite work of art, painstakingly planned, amazingly executed.

"Dad..."

I could hear them crossing around the garage to the side of the house. I knew they were curious, but I still didn't trust my voice. I looked back down at the leaf. Part of me wanted to reach out and touch it. Another part felt it was too sacred.

"Paul, what's wrong?"

"It's the leaf, isn't it." Ally's words were more a statement than a question. "He painted the leaf, didn't he?"

I said nothing as my eyes filled with moisture. I wasn't sure how she had known. Then again, the two always had that connection.

Yes, my father had finally created his masterpiece. At last he had been able to capture the love of God in his painting. Despite the cold winter nights, he had come up here to paint. Despite his growing cough, his declining health, he returned here, night after night, painting and repainting, until he finally got it right, until it was perfect, down to the tiniest detail. And he did it all for the love of another.

It was true. In more ways than I had dreamed possible, Dad had finally captured the love of his Savior.

Epilogue

IT WAS MID-DECEMBER, NEARLY NINE MONTHS FROM THE MORNing we first discovered the painting. I had just awakened in the middle of the night and sensed that something wasn't right. I lay there in the stillness, listening, but could only hear Jen's soft rhythmic breathing. I rolled over and glanced at the radio alarm. Its numbers burned a red 5:48. Beyond the clock came a faint glow from under our door. Somebody was up.

With a sigh, I slipped out from under the quilt and shuffled in my bare feet across the braided throw rug to the door. The brass knob felt cold as I opened it. Ally's bedroom light was burning . . . and the hallway light . . . and the stairway light . . . and who knew how many more lights downstairs. It made no difference how often I nagged at the kids to turn off the lights, they always forgot.

I stepped into the hallway and ambled toward Ally's room. But she wasn't there. She'd been home from the university nearly a week, and this was the first time I could remember her being out of bed before noon. I passed by her window and, as I always did, looked out. The leaf was still there, although, after a brutal summer sun, its colors were faded, even under the blue-gray glow of the streetlight.

I snapped off Ally's nightstand lamp and methodically followed her trail, switching off one light after another as I headed down the hall, down the steps, and into the living room.

Much had changed with us over the past nine months ... and much had not. For me, I suppose the greatest change came in understanding the power of being broken. It had taken a while for me to realize that the breaking was not God's discipline but His blessing. What a paradox: Our blessing lay in our breaking. Yet that's what it was. Oh, I still had my battles, believe me, but from that day of giving up and being broken, something had changed. I was freer, I was able to serve less fearfully, less self-consciously. And, broken, there was more of me to give and share with others.

Taking the five loaves and the two fish and looking up to heaven, he gave thanks and broke them.

That's what had happened. The Lord had taken the meager little gift of me, had broken it, and was now able to use it to bless and feed others. For the first time I could remember, my ministry was starting to have the same impact upon folks that (dare I say it?) Dad's always seemed to have. Not all at once, but gradually, day by day, I discovered my words were becoming more true, my counsel more wise, my service more meaningful.

I continued, following the trail of lights from the living room into the kitchen. Still no Ally. I noticed through the back-door window that the porch light was on, reflecting faint wisps of blowing snow. Looking out, I saw blackened footsteps leading down the sidewalk toward the garage. Angry with myself for not putting on my slippers, much less a coat, I braced for the cold and opened the back door. The air was biting. I moved gingerly down the sidewalk, trying to keep my feet off the freezing concrete as much as possible. I threw open the side garage door and quickly stepped in.

There was Ally in her sweats, standing in front of Dad's easel. She held a brush and palette and her face was scrunched into a frown. I knew she'd been having a hard time at school, and since she could no longer use dance as an artistic outlet, she'd been trying everything from ceramics to poetry to learning the guitar.

I glanced about the studio, grateful that she'd turned on the heater. "Hey," I said, shutting the door and rubbing life back into my hands.

"Hey," she said, obviously preoccupied.

I approached and moved around her for a better look. "I didn't know you painted."

"I don't," she scowled. "Not yet."

I looked at the canvas. "I don't know . . . that's a pretty good-looking crab, if you ask me."

She threw me a look. "It's supposed to be a hand."

"Oh . . . a hand." I squinted, trying to see it. "You sure?"

"Of course, I'm sure."

"Then what's this red circle here, isn't that like its head or something?"

"It's a wound, Father. It's Christ's nail-pierced hand. And these," she pointed to what I thought were legs, "these are his fingers, and that's his thumb."

"Oh. . . ," I said, still unable to see it, knowing she'd have better luck if she went for the crab (but having the good sense to keep such observations to myself). Instead, I stood quietly and watched as she continued painting.

Nearly a minute passed before she spoke again. "I've decided to drop out of the university."

"You what?" I couldn't hide the concern in my voice.

"Maybe I'll go to a Bible college first."

If I was surprised before, I was shocked now. "Why?"

"All they do at college is talk about quadratic equations, or stratified rock from the Paleozoic Period, or Keats' ode to some flowerpot."

"It's called an education, Ally."

"But what good does it do? I mean, here we've got a world destroying itself, billions of people who don't even know about God's love, and I'm studying calculus? What good is that?"

I said nothing, desperately trying to catch up to her logic but, as usual, she didn't wait. "Bethel College is only half an hour away. I figure I could commute, save some money, and maybe help you out with the youth—you know, run the high-school ministry or something. No offense, but those guys are real goofs, and they definitely need some sort of role model to whip them into shape. I mean, isn't that how you started out with Grandpa?"

I tried to swallow the sudden tightness growing in my throat.

"You okay?" she asked.

I nodded.

"I can always go to the university later. You sure you're okay? Looks like you got something in your eye."

"Yeah," I croaked, giving it a quick rub.

She continued to voice her thoughts. "I mean, I haven't made a final decision or anything. And I want to talk to you guys. But if it's God's will for me to leave, I should leave, shouldn't I? I mean, if it's God's will?"

I took a quick, shallow breath. "Yeah, if it's God's will."

The silence resumed. As usual, she had no idea what she'd just done to me. I watched as she continued to paint, as the hand grew no closer to looking like a hand.

When I finally trusted my voice, I spoke, trying to sound as casual as possible. "Listen, why don't I go fix us some breakfast. When it's ready, you can come in, and we'll talk some more."

"Whatever," she shrugged and continued to paint.

I nodded and waited another moment. When I realized I'd been dismissed, I started toward the door, then turned back to her again. "Give me about twenty minutes, okay?"

But she didn't hear. She was too involved in the painting.

After breakfast she would come back out and work on it again. She would work on it throughout the day, and she would work on it long into the night. That was her way. That would always be the way of my Ally.

Then Comes Marriage

ANGELA HUNT AND BILL MYERS

It's the morning of their first wedding anniversary, and they've had the worst fight of their lives. Will Heather and Kurt Stone make it through even one more year?

As a furious Heather unloads her marital woes on her mother, a bewildered and resentful Kurt heads for the racquetball court to vent his frustration. Now the real issue emerges: Kurt is a man, and Heather is a woman. How can two people wired so differently ever become one flesh? Or could the strength of their union lie in their very differences?

Best-selling authors Bill Myers and Angela Hunt spin a warm, humorous, insightful tale of young matrimony. From both a man's and a woman's point of view, here is the rose of marital bliss, complete with thorns. As Kurt and Heather individually revisit the befores and afters of their wedding, they strengthen their commitment and begin to redefine their love in wiser, less selfish terms.

Their awakening to the realities of marriage, and their coming to terms with each other's uniqueness are the story of every husband and wife. Lovingly crafted, *Then Comes Marriage* is a delightful novella filled with fond memories for seasoned couples and wisdom and encouragement for newlyweds.

Hardcover 0-310-23016-0
Audio Pages™, *Then Comes Marriage/Seaside* 0-310-23464-6

Pick up a copy today at your favorite bookstore!

Eli

BILL MYERS

What if Jesus had not come until today? Who would follow him? Who would kill him?

A fiery car crash hurls TV journalist Conrad Davis into another world exactly like ours except for one detail—Jesus Christ did not come 2,000 years ago, but today.

Starting with angels heralding a birth in the back of a motel laundry room, the skeptical Davis watches the gospel unfold in today's society as a Messiah in T-shirt and blue jeans heals, raises people from the dead, and speaks such startling truths that he captures the heart of a nation.

But the young man's actions and his criticism of the religious establishment earn him enemies as ruthless as they are powerful.

An intense and thought-provoking novel, *Eli* strips away religious tradition to present Jesus fresh and unvarnished. With gripping immediacy, Bill Myers weaves a story whose truth will refresh your faith.

Softcover 0-310-21803-9
Audio Pages™ 0-310-23622-3

Pick up a copy today at your favorite bookstore!

Blood of Heaven

BILL MYERS

Mysterious blood has been found on the remains of an ancient religious artifact. Some believe it is the blood of Christ. And experiments with specific genes from the blood have brought surprising findings. Now it's time to introduce those genes into a human.

Enter Michael Coleman: multiple killer, death row resident … and, if he is willing, human guinea pig. There are no promises. The effects may kill Coleman or completely destroy his sanity.

Follow Michael through the pages of this carefully researched science and psychological thriller that looks deep into the heart of man. Meet for the first time Katherine and Eric Lyon, the spellbinding characters from *Fire of Heaven*.

Softcover 0-310-20119-5
Audio Pages™ 0-310-21053-4

Pick up a copy today at your favorite bookstore!

Fire of Heaven

BILL MYERS

In this riveting sequel to *Blood of Heaven* and *Threshold*, Brandon Martus and Sarah Weintraub follow God's calling—right into danger.

This is not another end-times thriller, but one of the most intense and thought-provoking pieces of Christian fiction to come along in years. As the couple prepare for the final showdown against Satan himself, they must live and proclaim the truths Christ has given his end-times church. From America to Jerusalem, Brandon and Sarah battle the forces of man and hell while learning the true cost of following Christ.

Follow Brandon and Sarah as they learn the importance of their God-given calling and struggle to fulfill what they are to do, all the while battling supernatural evil and forces beyond their control.

"I couldn't put Fire of Heaven *down. Bill Myers's writing is crisp, fast-paced, provocative, and laced headily with Scripture. A very compelling story."*

—Francine Rivers

Softcover 0-310-21738-5
Audio Pages™ 0-310-23002-0

Pick up a copy today at your favorite bookstore!

We want to hear from you. Please send your comments about this book to us in care of the address below. Thank you.

GRAND RAPIDS, MICHIGAN 49530

www.zondervan.com